Alexa's broke, and desperate to keep her family home. Nick is rich, and stands to inherit a major corporation. Getting married—in name only, of course—seems like the perfect solution. Sign on the dotted line and each of their problems go away, right?

Alexa and Nick are about to discover that when it comes to love, contracts are made to be broken—and hearts are made for a lifetime commitment.

PRAISE FOR JENNIFER PROBST AND

THE MARRIAGE BARGAIN

"Charming, fast-paced. . . . It will hook you and leave you begging for more!"

—Laura Kaye, bestselling author of *Hearts in Darkness*

"A beautiful story with characters that will stay with you forever."

—Candace Havens, bestselling author of *Take It Like a Vamp*

"Fiery and wild . . . it goes straight to your heart."

—*Maldivian Book Reviewers*

"Absolutely amazing! I couldn't put it down."

—*Bitten by Paranormal Romance*

"Highly amusing. . . . Jennifer Probst is an amazing author."

—*Fresh Fiction*

"Witty, sweet, and sexy . . . very enjoyable."

—*Bookish Temptations*

"Jennifer Probst is quickly turning into one of my favorite authors!"

—Susan Meier, author of *Nanny for the Millionaire's Twins*

The Marriage Bargain

Jennifer Probst

GALLERY BOOKS

New York   London   Toronto   Sydney   New Delhi

G

Gallery Books
A Division of Simon & Schuster, Inc.
1230 Avenue of the Americas
New York, NY 10020

This work was previously published by Entangled Publishing, LLC.

First Gallery Books trade paperback edition September 2012

GALLERY BOOKS and colophon are registered trademarks of Simon & Schuster, Inc.

For information about special discounts for bulk purchases, please contact Simon & Schuster Special Sales at 1-866-506-1949 or business@ simonandschuster.com

The Simon & Schuster Speakers Bureau can bring authors to your live event. For more information or to book an event contact the Simon & Schuster Speakers Bureau at 1-866-248-3049 or visit our website at www. simonspeakers.com.

Manufactured in the United States of America

10 9 8 7 6 5 4 3

Library of Congress Cataloging-in-Publication Data is available.

ISBN 978-1-4767-2536-9
ISBN 978-1-62266-903-5 (ebook)

To my mom.
You read my first romance manuscripts written on an
old-fashioned typewriter, and even read the love scenes. You
encouraged me to pursue my dreams and never believed it was
just a hobby. You supported me through good and bad, every day,
throughout the years. You inspired me to be a better person in this
lifetime. I am proud to be your daughter.
This one's for you, Mom.

Prologue

Thirteen years ago...

"Ready or not, here I come!"

Alexa tore her hands away from her eyes and spun around. The woods shimmered with an eerie silence, but she sensed her friends close by. Without hesitation she ran, her sneakers pounding over the brush and sticks as she whizzed in and out of the large pine trees. Her ears pricked as she caught the tail end of a giggle.

She headed toward the sound, but the echo threw her off and all she managed to surprise was a squirrel with a large nut. The cool shade lured her deeper. One quick check in Maggie's usual hiding spot only revealed a pile of leaves. Alexa slowed her pace and almost decided to turn when she heard a voice.

"A little old for hide and seek, aren't you?"

Alexa pivoted on her sneaker and glared at her best

friend's older brother. "It's fun." She dismissed him with a haughty sniff. They used to be close, until he suddenly woke up one day and decided she wasn't worth his time. He never talked to her, or snuck into her house for chocolate chip cookies, or told her raunchy jokes any longer. Seems only the older, silly, *busty* girls snagged his attention now. Who cared? She refused to follow him around like a little kid. "Anyway, you wouldn't understand. You never want to hang with us. What are you doing out here alone?"

He got up from the ground and walked toward her. Nick Ryan was sixteen years old and a pain in the butt. He made fun of everything she did, and pretended he had the right to play God just because he was two years older.

He stood on long, muscled legs. His hair curled around the top of his ears and over his forehead, and was an intriguing mix of colors, from pale brown to gold. Like her Chex cereal, Alexa thought. A combination of rice, wheat and corn. His face was all lean, angular curves, set off by a sulky lower lip that always intrigued her. Light brown eyes gleamed with intelligence and a hint of pain. Alexa knew what pain felt like. That was the only quality she related to.

Nick Ryan was a rich kid who kept to himself and seemed to have no friends. She always wondered how his sister, Maggie, had turned out so social.

"You should be careful in the woods, brat. You could get lost."

"I know my way around better than you."

He gave a dismissive shrug. "Probably do. You should have been a boy."

Her temper spiked. She clenched her fists at her sides and tossed her ponytail. "And you should have been a girl. Everyone knows you don't like to get your hands dirty, pretty boy."

Direct hit. He actually looked annoyed. "You should learn to act like a real girl."

"How so?"

"Make-up. Looking pretty. Kissing boys."

She'd never spend her precious pennies on lip-gloss. It was hard enough to afford anything new, let alone make-up or perfume. Alexa made a gagging sound. "Gross."

"Bet you never kissed anyone before."

She heard the taunting tone in his voice. At fourteen, most of her girlfriends had already had their first kisses—Maggie included—but the thought always made her stomach turn. She'd rather die than admit it to Nick. "Yes, I have."

"Who?"

"None of your beeswax. I'm outta here."

"I dare you."

Her sneaker stopped mid-flight. A sharp bird call cut through the air, and Alexa felt like she'd hit a turning point. She stuck out her chin. "Dare me to what?"

"Show me you can kiss."

Her stomach slid and her heartbeat thundered and her palms sweat. She made a face. "With you?"

"I knew it."

"Why would I want to kiss you? I hate you!"

"Okay, forget it. I just wanted to see if you were a real girl. Now I know you're not."

His words sliced through her. All the doubt and uncertainty bubbled up inside and confirmed she was different. Why wasn't she like Maggie? Why did she prefer painting and reading and animals to boys? Maybe Nick was right and she was deficient. Maybe…

He started to walk away.

"Wait!"

He stood with his back toward her for a few moments, as if considering her plea. Slowly, he turned around. "What?"

She forced herself to close the distance and stopped in front of him. Her legs shook. Her body felt funny. Almost like she was going to throw up. "I know how to kiss. And I'll…I'll show you."

"Fine. Go ahead." He cocked his hip in an arrogant stance like he did this every day and was already getting bored.

Drawing on her knowledge from the movies, she leaned forward. *I will not screw this up. Relax my lips. Deep breath. Angle my head more to the side so we don't bump noses. God, what if I hit his chin and make him bleed? No, don't think about that. Kissing is a piece of cake.*

No big deal. No big deal. No big deal…

His breath was light and warm as it rushed over her lips. She arched her neck upward and paused. Then his lips touched hers.

She barely felt the brush but an array of sensations passed over her. The touch of his fingers over her shoulders. The gentle pressure of his mouth. The earthy scent of the woods mixed with a teasing hint of cologne.

In those few moments, he'd given her a rare gift. Her heart

burst open and a strange elation soared through her veins. Her first real kiss. How long had she dreaded and feared the experience, horribly afraid she'd hate boys and kissing and not be normal? She knew then she was a mature girl and would never question that part of herself again.

He slowly pulled away and her eyes drifted open. Their gazes met and locked. Her emotions poured through her in roaring, choppy waves, like she was zooming down the log ride at Great Adventure, and hung on with fear and excitement. She held her breath and waited.

An odd expression crossed his face. He studied her as if he'd never seen her before. For one glorious moment, she glimpsed something deep within his golden brown eyes—a shred of vulnerability he never shared. His lips curved in a hint of a smile.

She smiled back. Felt safe. Knew he wouldn't make fun of her or ignore her any longer. Things changed. What she denied and protested for so long suddenly popped out of her mouth without thought or consequence.

"I'm going to marry you one day."

She never questioned his response, confident in their friendship and their kiss. She trusted him with a bone deep knowledge. Alexa waited for his smile to grow larger, waited for his agreement, waited for their entire relationship to finally change after that one perfect kiss.

A shutter slammed over his face and the boy she kissed seemed to disappear.

Then Nick laughed.

She blinked, not understanding his reaction, but when her gaze once again met his, coldness seeped into her chest.

"Marry? Oh, that's a good one, Al. When I get married it'll be to a real woman. Not a child." He shook his head in sheer mockery, as if the thought would keep him amused for days on end. For laughs with his buddies. And his real girlfriends.

She stood there in the woods, only able to watch in horror, for once not able to make a smart mouth comeback.

His humor eased to a chuckle. "You got potential, though. With a little practice, you might get good at this kissing thing. See ya, kid."

He walked away.

A giggle rose through the air. With slow horror, she turned and caught one of her friends hidden in the bushes. Now everyone would know.

In that moment, on the brink of womanhood, she made her first decision: she'd never let Nick or any other boy humiliate her again. The only love worth counting on was family and friends. Boys could not be trusted, and she was smart enough not to need another lesson.

She turned and ran, hide and go seek forgotten, and wondered what the ache in her chest was.

Of course, she was still too young to pinpoint the actual cause.

Years later, she'd finally understand.

Her heart had been broken.

Chapter One

She needed a man.

Preferably one with $150,000 to spare.

Alexandria Maria McKenzie stared into the small homemade campfire in the middle of her living room floor and wondered if she had officially lost her mind. The piece of paper in her hand held all the qualities she dreamed her soul mate would possess. Loyalty. Intelligence. Humor. A strong sense of family and a love for animals. A healthy income.

Most of her ingredients were already cooking. One hair from a male family member—her brother was still pissed. A mix of scented herbs—probably to give him a tender side. And the small stick for…well, she hoped that didn't mean what she feared.

With a deep breath, she threw the list into the silver bucket and watched it burn. She felt like an idiot for creating a love spell, but she had no options left and little to lose. As the owner of an eclectic bookstore in a trendy upstate New York college town, she figured she was allowed some quirks. Like sending up a prayer to Earth Mother for the perfect man.

Alexa reached over and grabbed the fire extinguisher as the flames leaped. The smoke rose and reminded her of the burned pizza crust on the bottom of her toaster oven. She crinkled her nose, shot the spray into the middle of her carpet, and went to hunt up a glass of red wine to celebrate.

Her mom would have to sell Tara.

Her family home.

Alexa grabbed a bottle of Cabernet Sauvignon and thought about her dilemma. Her bookstore was mortgaged to the hilt. The café expansion would take careful planning, and there wasn't a dime to spare. She looked over the Victorian loft apartment and easily calculated there was nothing to sell. Not even on eBay.

She was twenty-seven and probably should live in a stylish condo, with designer clothes and a date every weekend. Instead, she took in homeless dogs from the local shelter and bought chic scarves to update her outfits. She believed in living in the sunlight, being open to every possibility, and following her heart. Unfortunately, none of those traits would save her mother's house.

She took a sip of the ruby red wine and acknow-ledged there was nothing left to do. No one had enough money, and this time when the tax collector came, there wouldn't be a happy ending. She was no Scarlett O'Hara. And Alexa didn't think her last-ditch attempt to make a love spell to lure the perfect man to her door was going to help.

The doorbell rang.

Her mouth fell open. My God, was it him? She looked at her grungy sweatpants and cropped shirt and wondered if she had time to change. She got up to rummage through the closet, but the bell rang again, so she walked over, took a deep breath, and reached for the knob.

"About time you answered the door."

Her hopes plummeted. Alexa stared at her best friend, Maggie Ryan, and scowled. "You were supposed to be a man."

Maggie snorted and walked in. She waved a hand in the air, flashing cherry red nails, and flopped onto the sofa. "Yeah, keep dreaming. You scared your last date off, so I won't be setting you up again. What happened here?"

"What do you mean I scared him? I thought he was going to attack me."

Maggie raised a brow. "He leaned in to give you a good-night kiss. You stumbled and fell on your ass, and he felt like an idiot. People kiss after a date, Al. It's a ritual thing."

Alexa tossed the remaining trash into a bag and scooped up the bucket. "He had tons of garlic at dinner and I didn't want him near me."

Maggie grabbed the wine glass and took a healthy swig. She stretched out long legs clad in black leather and hooked her high-heeled boots over the edge of the battered table. "Remind me again why you haven't had sex in the last decade?"

"Witch."

"Celibate."

Alexa gave up and laughed. "Okay, you win. Why are you gracing me with your presence on a Saturday night? You look good."

"Thanks. I'm meeting someone for drinks at eleven. Wanna come?"

"On your date?"

Maggie made a face and drained the rest of the glass. "You'll be better company. He's a bore."

"Why are you going out with him?"

"He looks good."

Alexa dropped next to her on the couch and sighed. "I wish I could be like you, Maggie. Why do I have so many hang-ups?"

"Why don't I have any?" Maggie's lips twisted in self-deprecating humor, then she pointed to the bucket. "So, what's the deal with the fire?"

Alexa sighed. "I was creating a love spell. To, uh…get a man."

Her friend threw back her head and laughed. "Okay. What's that have to do with the bucket?"

Alexa's cheeks flamed. She'd never live this down. "I made a fire to honor the Earth Mother," she whispered.

"Oh my God."

"Hear me out. I'm desperate. I still haven't met Mr. Right and another small problem came up I need to solve, so I combined both my needs into one list."

"What kind of list?"

"One of my customers told me she bought this book on

love spells, and when she made a list of all the qualities she was looking for in a man, he showed up."

Now Maggie looked interested. "A man appeared in her life with all the things she wanted?"

"Yep. The list has to be specific. It can't be too general, or supposedly the universe gets confused with your desires and sends nothing. She said if you follow the spell, the right man will appear."

Maggie's green eyes gleamed. "Let me see the book."

Nothing like another single female to make you feel better about the quest for a man. Alexa tossed her the little fabric-covered book, feeling less like an idiot.

"Hmmm. Show me your list."

She waved toward the bucket. "Burned it."

"I know you have another copy under your bed. Forget it, I'll get it myself." Her friend stalked off toward the canary yellow futon and stuck her hand under the cushions. Within seconds she held the list triumphantly between bright red fingernails and licked her lips as if she was about to dive into a lusty romance novel. Alexa settled on the carpet and slumped over. Let the humiliation begin.

"Number one," Maggie recited. "A Mets fan."

Alexa braced herself for the explosion.

"Baseball?" Maggie shrieked. She waved the paper back and forth in the air for dramatic effect. "Damn it, how can you make your number one priority *baseball*? They haven't made it to the World Series in years! It's a fact in New York there are more Yankees fans than Mets fans, and that wipes out most of the male population."

Alexa gritted her teeth. Why was she constantly barraged over her choice of New York teams? "The Mets have heart and character, and I need a man who can root for the underdog. I refuse to sleep with a Yankees fan."

"You're hopeless. I give up," Maggie said. "Number two: loves books, art, and poetry."

She paused to think about it, then shrugged. "I accept. Three: believes in monogamy. Very important to the list. Number four: wants children." She looked up. "How many?"

Alexa smiled at the thought. "I'd like three. But I'd settle for two. Should I have specified how many in the list?"

"No, Earth Mother will get it right." Maggie continued. "Number five: knows how to communicate with a woman. Good one. I'm sick of reading books about Venus and Mars. I've gone through the whole series and I still don't have a clue. Number six: loves animals." She groaned. "That's as bad as the Mets!"

Alexa scooted around on the carpet to face her. "If he hates dogs, how can I continue my volunteer program at the shelter? And what if he's a hunter? I'd wake up in the middle of the night and find a dead deer staring at me from over the mantelpiece."

"You're so dramatic." Maggie turned back to the list. "Number seven: has a moral code of ethics and believes in honesty. Should've been number one on the list, but what the hell, I'm not a Mets fan. Number eight: a good lover." She waggled her eyebrows. "That would be number two on my list. But I'm proud the item even showed up. Maybe you're not as hopeless as I thought."

Alexa swallowed hard, dread curling her insides. "Keep going."

"Number nine: has a strong sense of family. Makes sense — you guys remind me of the frickin' *Waltons*. Okay, number ten…"

The clock ticked. Alexa watched Maggie read the item again.

"Alexa, I think I'm reading number ten wrong."

Alexa sighed. "Probably not."

Maggie recited the last request. "Needs one hundred and fifty thousand dollars available cash." She looked up. "I need more details."

Alexa lifted her chin. "I need a man I can love, with an extra one hundred and fifty thousand thrown in. And I need him fast."

Maggie shook her head like she surfaced from underwater. "For what?"

"To save Tara."

Maggie blinked. "Tara?"

"Yeah, my mother's home. You know, like in the movie *Gone with the Wind*? Remember how my mom used to joke about needing more cotton to pay the bills? I haven't told you how bad it's gotten, Maggs. Mom wants to sell and I can't let her. They have no money and nowhere else to go. I'll do anything to help, even marry. Just like Scarlett."

Maggie moaned and grabbed her purse. She ripped out her phone and punched in some numbers.

"What are you doing?" Alexa fought panic at the thought her best friend wouldn't understand. After all, she'd never asked for a man to solve her problems before. Oh, how the mighty had fallen.

"Canceling my date. I think this new item needs to be discussed. Then I'm calling my therapist. She's very good, discreet, and she takes midnight appointments."

Alexa laughed. "You're such a good friend, Maggie."

"Yeah, tell me about it."

. . .

Nicholas Ryan had a fortune at his fingertips.

But to get the one thing he wanted, he needed a wife.

Nick believed in many things. Working hard to accomplish a goal. Controlling anger and resorting to reason when a moment became confrontational. And creating buildings. Buildings that were solid yet aesthetically beautiful. Smooth angles and sharp lines blending together. Bricks and concrete and glass attesting to the solidity that people craved in ordinary life. The short moment of wonder when a person looks upon the final creation for the first time. All of these things made sense to him.

Nick did not believe in love everlasting, marriage, and family. These things made no sense, and he had decided not to incorporate such societal themes into his life.

Unfortunately, Uncle Earl had changed the rules.

Nick's gut coiled, and his sick sense of humor almost caused a laugh to spill from his lips. He rose from his leather chair and stripped off his navy jacket, striped silk tie, and snowy white shirt. One flick of his wrist unbuckled his belt, and he quickly changed into a pair of gray sweatpants and matching T-shirt. He thrust both feet into his Nike Air sneakers and entered his office's inner sanctum, which he'd filled with models, sketches, inspiring photos, a treadmill, some weights, and a fully stocked bar. He hit the button on the remote for the MP3 player. The strains of *La Traviata* filled the room and cleared his head.

He turned on the treadmill and tried not to think of smoking. Even after five years, when the stress kicked up a notch, he longed for a cigarette. Annoyed at his weakness when the urge hit, he exercised. Running soothed him, especially in his perfectly controlled environment. No loud voices interrupting his concentration, no scorching sunlight, no rocks or gravel impeding his path. He set the panel and began the steady pace that would lead him toward a solution.

Even though he understood his uncle's intentions, the sense of betrayal slowly ate away at his peace. In the end, one of the only family members he loved had used him as a pawn.

Nick shook his head. He should have seen this coming. Uncle Earl had spent his last few months spouting the importance of family and had thought Nick's response was lackluster. Nick wondered why his uncle was surprised. After all, his family should have been an advertisement for birth control.

As Nick had drifted in and out of relationships, one thing became clear—all women wanted marriage, and marriage meant messiness. Fights about emotion. Children tearing them both at the seams, wanting more attention. Needing more space, until the end became the same as every other relationship. Divorce. With children as the casualties.

No thanks.

He pumped up the incline and adjusted the speed as his thoughts whirled. Uncle Earl remained stubbornly optimistic until the bitter end that a woman would save his nephew's life. The heart attack had struck hard and fast. When the lawyers finally descended like a pack of vultures on the scent of blood money, Nick thought the legalities would be easy. His sister, Maggie, had already made it quite clear she wanted nothing to do with the business. Uncle Earl had no other relatives. So, for the first time, Nick believed in good fortune. Finally, he'd have something completely his own.

Until the lawyers read the will.

Then he realized the joke was on him.

He would inherit the majority of the Dreamscape shares as soon as he married. The marriage must last for one year, to any woman he chose, and a prenuptial agreement was acceptable. If Nick decided not to comply with his uncle's wishes, he'd retain 51 percent; the balance would be split among the board members, and Nick would be nothing but a figurehead. Instead of creating buildings, he'd be stuck in meetings and corporate politics—exactly what he did not want to do with his life.

And Uncle Earl had known it.

So now Nick had to find a wife.

He hit the switch and the incline lowered. He slowed his pace and evened his breath. With methodical precision, his mind cut through the emotional emptiness and scanned the possibilities. He got off the treadmill, grabbed a chilled bottle of Evian from the minibar, and walked back to his chair. He took a swallow of the icy, clean liquid and placed the sweating bottle on his desk. Waited a few minutes as he gathered his thoughts. Then picked up the gold pen and rolled it between his fingers.

He printed the words, each a nail banged into his own personal coffin.

Find a wife.

He wouldn't waste any more time griping about unfairness. Nick decided to make a clear list of the attributes his wife would need, and then see if he could think of any appropriate candidates.

Immediately, an image of Gabriella arose, but he squashed the thought. The stunning supermodel he currently dated was perfect for social functions and great sex, but not marriage. Gabriella was a sharp conversationalist and he enjoyed her company, but he was afraid she was already falling in love with him. She'd hinted at her desire to have children, which was a deal breaker. No matter how he laid out the ground rules of a marriage, emotion would ruin it. She'd become jealous and demanding, like any normal wife. No prenup would ever stand up to her greed once she felt betrayed.

He took another drink of water and ran his thumb in circles over the rough edge of the bottle top. He'd once read if a person made a list of all the qualities he admired in a woman, one appeared. Nick frowned as he grabbed at the fleeting thought. He was almost positive the theory had something to do with the universe. Getting back what you put into the cosmos. Some metaphysical crap he didn't believe in.

But today he was desperate.

He set the pen on the left edge of the page and wrote his list.

A woman who does not love me.

A woman I do not desire to sleep with.

A woman who does not have a big family.

A woman who does not have any animals.

A woman who does not want any children.

A woman who has an independent career.

A woman who will view the relationship as a business venture.

A woman who is not overly emotional or impulsive.

A woman I can trust.

Nick read over the summary. He knew some of his desired qualities were stubbornly optimistic, but if the universe theory worked, he might as well put down everything he wanted. He needed a woman who looked upon the venture as a business opportunity. Perhaps someone who craved a large payoff. He intended to offer many fringe benefits, but he wanted the marriage in name only. No sex equals no jealousy. No overly emotional woman equals no love.

No messiness equals a perfect marriage.

He sifted through each woman he'd dated in his past, every female friend he'd exchanged words with, every business associate he'd ever lunched with.

He came up with nothing.

Frustration nibbled on the edges of his nerves. He was a thirty-year-old man, reasonably attractive, intelligent, and financially secure. And he couldn't come up with one decent woman to marry.

He had one week to find his wife.

His cell phone rang. Nick picked it up. "Ryan."

"Nick, it's me. Maggie." She paused. "Did you find a wife yet?"

A chuckle strangled his lips. His sister was the only woman in the world who got him to laugh on a regular basis. Even if it was sometimes at his expense. "Working on it now."

"I think I found her."

His heartbeat sped up. "Who is it?"

Another pause. "You'd have to meet her terms, but I don't think they'll be a problem. Be open-minded. I know that's not your forte. But you can trust her."

He checked the last item on his list. A strange buzzing hummed in his ears as if in warning of his sister's next words. "Who is it, Maggs?"

Silence fell over the line for a beat. "Alexa."

The room whirled in a dizzying blur at the familiar name from his past. His only thought flashed like a mantra in vivid neon, over and over.

No frickin' way.

Chapter Two

Nick glanced around, satisfied with the result. His private conference room provided a business atmosphere, and the bouquet of fresh flowers his secretary had placed in the center of the table offered a personal touch amongst the plush wine carpeting, the rich gleam of cherrywood, and the buttery leather chairs. The contracts were neatly laid out, along with an elegant silver tray filled with tea, coffee, and a variety of pastries. Formal, yet friendly—which would reflect the tone of their marriage.

He ignored the pitch deep in his gut when he thought of encountering Alexandria McKenzie again. He wondered how she'd grown. The stories his sister shared with him painted a picture of a reckless, impulsive woman. He'd initially balked at Maggie's suggestion—Alexa didn't fit the image he needed. Stubborn memories of a free-spirited kid with a ponytail bobbing teased his thoughts; however, he knew she owned a respectable bookstore. He still thought of her as Maggie's playmate, even though he hadn't seen her in years.

But time was running out.

They shared a distant past, and he sensed Alexa could be trusted. She may not fit his idea of the perfect wife, but she needed money. Fast. Maggie remained silent regarding the reason, but she painted Alexa as desperate. A need for cash he was comfortable with—it was black and white. No gray areas. No ideas of intimacy between them. A formal business transaction between old friends. Nick could live with that.

He reached for the intercom to buzz his secretary, but the heavy door smoothly swung open at the same time and closed with a solid *click*.

He turned.

Deep blue eyes cut straight to his with little hesitation and a clearness that told him this woman would lose any poker game—she was brutally honest and unwilling to bluff. He recognized her gaze well enough, but age had changed the colors to a disturbing mix of aquamarine and sapphire. Certain images came to mind—plumbing the depths of the Caribbean Sea in search of its mysteries. A canvas of Sinatra's umbrella skies stretched so far and wide a man couldn't find the beginning or end.

Her eyes were startling against the inky black of her hair, which consisted of corkscrew curls that tumbled past her shoulders and framed her face with a natural wildness she seemed unable to tame. High cheekbones set off a lush mouth. He used to ask her if she'd been stung by a bee, then crack up laughing. The joke was on him. Hot male fantasies were built around a mouth like hers—and it had nothing to do with bees. Just honey. Preferably warm, sticky honey poured over those plump lips and slowly licked off.

Ah, hell.

He reined himself in and finished his inspection. He remembered torturing her when he found out she had to wear a bra. An early developer, she'd been mortified by his discovery, and he'd used the information to hurt her. Now, it wasn't funny anymore. Her breasts were as lush as her mouth, and they matched the curve of her hips. She was tall, almost as tall as he, and this package of female temptation came all wrapped up in a fiery red tank dress that emphasized her cleavage, skimmed over her hips, and fell to the floor. Scarlet toenails peeked through shiny red sandals. She remained still in the doorway, as if allowing him to drink his fill before she decided to speak.

Feeling somewhat staggered, Nick fought past his discomposure and relied on professionalism to hide his reaction. Alexandria Maria McKenzie had grown up well. A little too well for his taste. But there was no need to let her know.

He offered her the same neutral smile he'd offer any business associate. "Hello, Alexa. It's been a long time."

She smiled back but it didn't reach her eyes. She shifted her feet and fisted her hands. "Hello, Nick. How are you?"

"Fine. Please sit down. Can I pour you coffee? Tea?"

"Coffee, please."

"Cream? Sugar?"

"Cream. Thank you." She slid gracefully into the cushioned chair, swiveled away from the desk, and crossed her legs. The slinky red material crept up and gave him a glimpse of her legs, smooth and athletic.

He concentrated on the coffee. "Napoleon? Apple fritter? They're from the bakery across the street."

"No, thank you."

"Sure?"

"Yes. I'd never be able to stop at one. I've learned not to tempt myself."

The word *tempt* fell from her lips in a low, smoky voice that stroked his ears. His pants tightened a notch and he realized her voice stroked other places as well. Completely disconcerted by his reaction to a woman he wanted no physical contact with, he focused on preparing her coffee and sat across from her.

They studied each other for a few moments and the silence lengthened. She plucked at the delicate gold bracelet encircling her wrist. "I'm sorry about your uncle Earl."

"Thank you. Did Maggie fill you in on the details?"

"The whole thing sounds crazy."

"It is. Uncle Earl believed in family, and before he died he was convinced I'd never settle down. Therefore, he decided a strong push would be for my own good."

"You don't believe in marriage?"

He shrugged. "Marriage is unnecessary. The dream of forever is a fairy tale. White knights and monogamy don't exist."

She drew back in surprise. "You don't believe in making a commitment to another person?"

"Commitments are short-lived. Sure, people mean it when they confess love and devotion, but time erodes all the good stuff and leaves the bad. Do you know anyone who is happily married?"

She parted her lips, then lapsed into silence. "Besides my parents? I guess not. But that doesn't mean there aren't happy couples."

"Maybe." His tone contradicted his partial agree-ment.

"I guess there are a lot of issues we don't agree upon," she said, and then shifted in her seat and re-crossed her legs. "We'll need some time together to see if this thing will work."

"We have no time. The wedding has to take place by the end of next week. It doesn't matter if we get along. This is strictly a business arrangement."

She narrowed her eyes. "I see you're the same overbearing bully who teased me about my chest size. Some things don't change."

He focused his attention on the dip of her dress. "I guess you're right. Some things remain the same. Others keep expanding."

Her breath caught at the jab, but she surprised him when she smiled. "And other things remain small." Her pointed stare settled directly on the bulge in the center of his pants.

Nick almost sputtered into his coffee but managed to set the cup down with calm dignity. A rush of heat punched his gut as he remembered the day in the pool when they were kids.

He had been teasing Alexa mercilessly about the changes in her body when Maggie snuck up behind him and yanked down his swim trunks. Exposed in all senses of the word, he'd stalked away and pretended the whole episode didn't bother him. But the memory still ranked as his most embarrassing moment.

He motioned to the papers in front of her. "Maggie told me you needed a specific amount of money. I kept the figure open for negotiation."

An odd expression crossed her face. Her features tightened, then smoothed back out. "Is this the contract?"

He nodded. "I know you'll need your lawyer to look it over."

"No need. A friend of mine is a lawyer. I learned enough, since I helped him study for the bar exam. May I see it?"

He slid the papers over the polished wood. She reached in her purse for a pair of small black reading glasses and pushed them up the bridge of her nose. Minutes passed as she studied the contract. He took the opportunity to study her. His strong attraction irritated him. Alexa wasn't his type. She was too curvy, too direct, too…real. He wanted to know he was safe from any emotional outbursts if something didn't go her way. Even when Gabby became upset, she always handled herself with restraint. Alexa scared the hell out of him. Something in his gut whispered she wouldn't be easy to handle. She spoke her opinion and exhibited emotions without thought. Such reactions caused danger and havoc and messiness. The last thing he needed in a marriage.

Yet…

He trusted her. Those sapphire eyes bespoke a certain

determination and fairness. Her promise meant something. After a year, he knew she'd walk away without a glance backward or a desire for more money. The scale tipped in her favor.

One cherry red fingernail tapped the edge of the page in a steady rhythm. She looked up. Nick wondered why her skin had taken on such a pale tone when she'd seemed so flushed and healthy a moment ago.

"You have a list of requirements?" She said it as if she were accusing him of a capital crime instead of making a list of assets and liabilities.

He cleared his throat. "Just a few qualities I'd like my wife to have." She opened her mouth to speak but no words emerged. She seemed to struggle to get them free.

"You want a hostess, an orphan, and a robot all rolled into one. Is that fair?"

He took a deep breath. "You're exaggerating. Just because I'd like to marry someone with grace and business sense doesn't mean I'm a monster."

"You want a Stepford wife without the sex. Haven't you learned anything about women since you were fourteen?"

"I learned plenty. That's why Uncle Earl had to force me into an institution that favors women in the first place."

She gasped. "Men get plenty out of marriage!"

"Like what?"

"Steady sex and companionship."

"After six months, the headaches start and you bore each other to tears."

"Someone to grow old with."

"Men never want to grow old. That's why they keep seeking out younger women."

Her mouth dropped open. She closed it with one quick snap. "Children…a family…someone who will love you in sickness and in health."

"Someone who spends all your money and nags you every night and bitches about cleaning up your mess."

"You're sick."

"You're deluded."

She shook her head, causing her silky black curls to lift around her face, then slowly settle. The flush was back in her skin. "God, your parents really screwed you up," she muttered.

"Thank you, Freud."

"What if I don't fit in all these categories?"

"We'll work on it."

Her eyes narrowed and she bit her lower lip. Nick flashed back to the first time he'd kissed her, when he was sixteen. How his mouth had pressed against hers, feeling her tremble. His fingers lightly caressing the bare skin of her shoulders. The fresh, clean scent of flowers and soap teasing his nostrils. Afterward, her features shone with innocence, beauty, purity. Waiting for the happily-ever-after part.

Then she had smiled and told him she loved him. Wanted to marry him. He should have patted her on the head, said something nice, and gone on his way. Instead, her marriage remark had been sweet and tempting in a way that had scared the crap out of him. Even at sixteen, Nick knew no relationship could ever be beautiful—they all eventually turned ugly. He'd laughed, called her a baby, and left her alone in the woods. The vulnerability and hurt in her face had tore at his heart, but he'd hardened himself to the emotion. The earlier she learned, the better.

Nick had made sure they both learned tough lessons that day.

He shook off the memory and concentrated on the present. "Why don't you tell me what you're looking for in this marriage?"

"One hundred and fifty thousand dollars. Cash. Up front and not at the end of the year."

He leaned closer to her, intrigued. "Hell of a lot of money. Gambling debts?"

An invisible wall slammed between them. "No."

"Shopping spree?"

Temper flared in her eyes. "None of your business. Part of the deal is that you ask me no questions about the money or how I intend to use it."

"Hmmm, anything else?"

"Where do we live?"

"My home."

"I'm not giving up my apartment. I'll pay the rent as usual."

Surprise shot through him. "As my wife, you'll need a proper wardrobe. You'll get an allowance and have access to my personal shopper."

"I'll wear what I want, when I want, and pay my own damn way."

He fought back a smile. He almost enjoyed the match of minds, just like he had in the old days. "You'll play hostess to my business associates. I have a huge deal on the line, so you'll need to make nice with the other wives."

"I can manage to keep my elbows off the table and laugh at their stupid jokes. But I need to be free to run my own business and enjoy my own social life."

"Of course. I expect you to carry on your individual lifestyle."

"As long as I don't embarrass you?"

"Exactly."

She tapped her toe in rhythm to her fingernails. "I've got some problems with this list."

"I'm a flexible person."

"I'm very close to my family and they'll need a good reason to believe I'm suddenly getting married."

"Just tell them we ran into each other after all these years and decided to marry."

Alexa rolled her eyes. "They're not allowed to know about this arrangement, so they need to believe we're madly in love. You'll have to come to dinner so we can make the announcement. And it needs to be convincing."

He remembered that her father had left them for the bottle and abandoned her family. "You still speak with your father?"

"Yes."

"You used to hate him."

"He's made amends. I chose to forgive. Anyway, my brother and sister-in-law and niece and the twins all live with my parents. They'll ask a million questions, so you have to be convincing."

He frowned. "I don't like complications."

"Tough luck. That's part of the deal."

Nick figured he'd give her the small victory. "Fine. Anything else?"

"Yeah. I get a real wedding."

His eyes narrowed. "I was thinking justice of the peace."

"I was thinking a white dress outside with my family in attendance and Maggie as maid of honor."

"I don't like weddings."

"So you've said. My family will never believe I eloped. We have to do this for them."

"I'm marrying you for business reasons, Alexa. Not your family."

Her chin tilted up. He made a mental note of the gesture. Seemed like a warning before she charged into battle. "Believe me, I'm not happy about this, either, but we have to play the part if people are going to think this is real."

His features tightened but he managed a nod. "Fine." His voice dripped with sarcasm. "Anything else?"

She looked a bit nervous as she shot him a glance, then rose from the chair and began pacing the room. His focus switched to her perfect rear end, swinging back and forth, and his zipper strained in discomfort.

His last fleeting rational thought skipped past his vision. *Cut your losses here and now and walk out the door. This woman is going to turn your life upside down, diagonal and sideways, and you've always hated the fun house.*

Nick fought the sudden surge of fear and waited for her answer.

• • •

Ah, hell.

Why did he have to be so damned gorgeous?

She snuck a glance at him as she paced. A vulgar curse rose to her lips but she forced it back down. Growing up, she used to sneer and call him Pretty Boy because of his golden hair. Those youthful curls had been tamed into a short, conservative cut, but some unruly strands fell across his brow in stubborn rebellion. The colors had deepened with time, but they still reminded her of Chex Mix cereal, ranging from honey blond to wheat. His features had hardened—his jaw was now slightly chiseled. Perfect white teeth flashed at her during that brief smile. His eyes were the same deep chestnut, and they hinted at veiled secrets kept firmly locked behind a wall. But his body...

He'd always been active, but when he crossed the room the elegant fabric of his oatmeal-colored pants moved and bent to his will, outlining long muscular legs and taut buttocks. The V-neck tan sweater was both casual and appropriate for the office on a Saturday.

Some parts were totally inappropriate. The corded length of his arms. The broad shoulders and chest that stretched and molded the fabric. The deep bronze of his skin, as if he had been lying in the sun for hours. The animal litheness of his movements. He had grown up, and he was no pretty boy. Nick Ryan was all hot-blooded man—and he still looked at her as Maggie's little playmate. When their eyes locked, there was no recognition, no appreciation. Just a distant friendliness afforded to someone from his past.

Well, she'd be damned if she let her tongue loll out of her mouth just because he was attractive. His personality still sucked. The big B for Boring. The big D for Dull. The big…

She pushed *that* thought out of her mind.

Alexa hated the fact that his presence made her nervous and a bit giddy. One week ago, she'd cast a love spell, and Earth Mother had listened. She had her money and could save her family's home. But what the hell had happened to her list?

The man before her struck out on everything she believed in. This was no love match. No, this was business, pure and simple, and so very cold. While her memory of their first kiss rose from the recesses of her mind, she bet he'd forgotten the moment completely. Humiliation wriggled through her. No more. Would Earth Mother really not allow her the number one requirement on her list? She took a deep breath and spoke. "One other thing."

"Yes?" he asked.

"Do you watch baseball?"

"Of course."

Her stomach pitched with tension. "Do you have a favorite team?"

He smirked. Literally *smirked*. "There's only one New York team."

Alexa fought past the nausea and asked the question. "Which one?"

"The Yankees, of course. They're the only team that wins. They're the only team that matters."

She took deep belly breaths, which she'd learned in yoga class. Could she marry a Yankees fan? Would she be giving up all her morals and ethics? Could she stand being married to a man who made logic his God and thought monogamy was a female thing?

"Alexa? Are you okay?"

She silenced him with one hand and paced, searching desperately for answers. If she walked out now, there was no other option but to sell the house. Could she live with herself, knowing she was too selfish to make a sacrifice for her family? Did she have a choice?

"Alexa?"

She spun on one heel. Impatience carved the lines of his face. This man had no tolerance for any emotional outbursts. As hot as he looked, he'd be one major pain in the ass, just as he had been growing up. He probably scheduled his days by the minute. He probably didn't know what the word *impulsive* meant. Could they make a year of living in the same house? Would they rip each other apart before 365 days passed? And what if the Yankees went to the World Series this year? She'd have to deal with his lousy arrogance and patronizing smiles. Oh God…

He crossed his arms in front of his chest. "Don't tell me. You're a Mets fan."

She shuddered at his tone. "I refuse to talk baseball with you. You will not wear any of your Yankees gear when you're with me. I don't care what you put on when I'm not around. Understand?"

Silence settled over the room. She risked a glance in his direction. He stared at her as if her hair had sprouted Medusa snakes. "Are you kidding me?"

She shook her head with gusto. "No."

"I'm not even allowed to wear my Yankees cap?"

"That's right."

"You're insane," he said.

"Sticks and stones. Tell me now before we waste any more time."

Then he did something she hadn't seen since the neighborhood bully fell off his bike and burst into silly feminine tears.

Nick Ryan laughed. Not a glimmer of amusement or a smirk around the lips. This was a no-holds belly laugh, deep and masculine. The sound filled the room and pumped it with life. Alexa fought back her own smile, especially since his humor was directed at her. Damn, he looked good when he got off his high horse.

He finally calmed, seemed to think the option over, and settled on a solution. "I won't wear any Yankees gear, but the same applies to you. No Mets junk. I don't even want to see a coffee mug or key chain lying around my house. Got it?"

She simmered with annoyance. Somehow, the deal had been turned around on her. "I disagree. We haven't won a Series since 1986, so I get to wear mine. You get enough glory—you don't need any more."

The corner of his lip twitched. "Nice try, but I'm not one of the Twinkies you're used to dating. No Yankees, no Mets. Take it or leave it."

"I don't date Twinkies!"

He shrugged. "I don't care."

She hopped from one foot to the other and barely

managed to keep her hands from curling into fists. He was so damn detached. How could he look so tasty, yet remind her of the poison apple Snow White was offered?

"Well? Do you want to sleep on it or whatever women do when they can't make a decision?"

She bit her lip, hard, and forced out the words. "Fine. You have a deal."

"Anything else?"

"I guess that covers it."

"Not quite." He paused as if about to approach a delicate topic. Alexa swore she'd remain calm, no matter what he said. Two could play this game. She'd be an ice queen, even if he verbally tortured her. She took a breath and slid back into the chair, then picked up her coffee cup to sip at the brew.

He steepled his fingers and took a breath. "I want to talk to you about sex."

"Sex?" The word dropped from her lips and fired into the air like a gunshot. She blinked but refused to show any change in expression.

He jumped from his seat and they switched places as he paced the luxurious burgundy carpet. "See, we need to be extremely discreet with, uh, our extracurricular activities."

"Discreet?"

"Yes. I deal with some very high-end clients, and I have a reputation to protect. Let alone the terms of the agreement would be broken if our marriage were questioned. I think it best if you agree to remain celibate for the year. It's doable, don't you think?"

"Or a lot of non-doing."

He gave an obvious fake laugh and she wondered if she caught a gleam of sweat on his forehead or if it were just a trick of the light. He stopped pacing and watched her almost warily. Suddenly, the true meaning of his words caught fire in her brain and the lightning rod of knowledge sizzled. Nick wanted her to be the perfect wife, which included holding a chaste marriage bed under their ruse.

But he hadn't mentioned his own celibacy. Maggie had spilled all the details about Gabriella, so she knew Nick was involved in a relationship. Alexa still didn't understand why he wouldn't marry his girlfriend, but his choice wasn't for her to judge. All she cared about was the chauvinistic male pig before her and her desire to call the whole deal off.

Almost.

She shook with anger but kept her face serene. Nick Ryan wanted to cut deals. Fine. Because when she walked out this door, Nicky would sign the deal of a lifetime.

She smiled. "I understand."

His face practically lit up. "You do?"

"Of course. If the marriage is supposed to be real, how would it look to find your wife the gossip of an affair so soon after the wedding?"

"Exactly."

"And you shouldn't have to deal with humiliating questions regarding your manhood. If your wife is sleeping around, it's obvious what the problem is. She wasn't getting it good enough at home."

He shifted his weight. His nod was halfhearted. "I guess."

"So, what about Gabriella?"

He drew back in surprise. "How do you know about her?"

"Maggie."

"Don't worry about Gabriella. I'll take care of her."

"Are you sleeping with her?"

He flinched, then tried to pretend he didn't care. "Does it matter?"

She lifted her hands in defense. "I want to clarify the sex issue. At least I've filled the number one and two spot. I sure as hell don't love you, and we're not attracted to each other. You're saying if I want to have a rollicking one-night stand, I can't go for it. So, what are the rules for you?"

Alexa pursed her lips and wondered how the man intended to get himself out of his freshly dug grave.

• • •

Nick stared at the woman before him and tried to swallow. Her smoky voice set off even smokier images of her naked and demanding and…rollicking. He bit off a curse and reached for more coffee, trying to buy some time. Her whole demeanor screamed sex. The innocence of youth had burned off and left behind a pure-blooded woman with pure-blooded needs. He wondered what kind of man satisfied those needs. He wondered how ripe her breasts would feel in his hands or how her lips would taste under his. He wondered what she wore under the clinging red dress.

"Nick?"

"Hmmm?"

"Did you hear me?"

"Yeah. Sex. I promise you'll never find yourself in an awkward situation."

"So, you're telling me you still intend to sleep with Gabriella?"

"Gabriella and I are involved in a relationship."

"But you won't marry her."

Tension snapped the air around them. He took a few steps away, desperate for some distance. "It's not that kind of relationship."

"Hmmm, interesting. So, you're saying I can't screw around because I don't have anybody steady to screw around with."

If ice cubes were available he would have sucked them down one by one. Her accusation made a strange heat rise to his skin. Her tone was mild. Her smile seemed easy and genuine. Nick felt poised on the edge of some female power trip, and he recognized he was on losing ground. He rallied for the upper hand.

"If you had someone steady in your life, we'd work out the situation. But strangers are too dangerous. I can guarantee Gabriella knows how to keep a secret."

She smiled then. A delicious, feminine smile that promised delights beyond imagination and promised it all to him. His heart stopped, paused, then went on beating. Fascinated, he waited for her next words.

"No way, baby."

He fought for concentration as her refusal slipped from that luscious mouth. "Pardon?"

"No sex for me. No sex for you. I don't care if it's Gabriella or a stripper or the love of your damn life. If I don't have any fun, you don't. You'll just have to get your kicks out of this very proper business marriage and build your buildings." She paused. "Get it?"

He got it. Decided not to accept it. And realized this was game, set, and match, and he needed to win. His smile promised compassion and understanding and the money she needed. "Alexa, I understand this doesn't seem fair. But a man is different. Gabriella has a reputation to uphold, also, so you'll never be put in a bad position. Do you understand?"

"Yes."

"So, you'll agree to the terms?"

"No."

Annoyance surged. He narrowed his eyes and studied her. Then decided to go for the close. "We've been able to agree on everything else. We've compro-mised. It's only one year, and then you can walk away and have a damn orgy for all I care."

Ice-blue eyes stared back at him with sheer stubbornness and steely determination. "If you get to have your orgies, I get mine. If you want to be celibate, so will I. I don't care about your crap regarding men and women and their differences. If I have to go to bed alone for three hundred and sixty-four nights, then so will you. And if you want action, you'll have to turn to your own wife."

She tossed her head like a stallion just out of the gate. "And since we know we're not attracted to each other, you'll just have to find some other ways to ease the pressure. Use a little creativity. Celibacy should open other outlets." She smiled. "'Cause that's all you're gonna get."

Obviously she had no idea he was a master poker player and had spent the past few years blowing off steam in games where night turned into day and he walked off thousands richer. Like his old smoking habit, poker called to him and he used the vice for pleasure, not profit.

He refused to let her beat him, and he sensed victory was close. He dove for the jugular. "You want to be unreasonable? Fine. Deal is off. Kiss your money good-bye. I'll just have to manage the board for a while."

She slid out of the chair, hooked her purse over her shoulder, and stood before him. "It was nice to see you again, Pretty Boy."

Direct hit.

He wondered if she knew how her mocking endearment irritated him and made him want to shake her until she took it back. Even as a kid, he'd hated it, and the years hadn't dulled the sharp edge of the insult. As he did when he was younger, he gritted his teeth and bore the annoyance with an easy grin. "Yeah, it was nice. Stop by some time. Don't be a stranger."

"I won't." She paused. "See ya."

That was the moment Nick knew he was wrong. Dead wrong. Alexandria Maria McKenzie could win at poker—not because she lied, but because she was willing to lose.

She also played a mean game of chicken.

She turned. Strode to the door. Twisted the knob. Then…

"Okay." The word fired out of his mouth before he had time to think. Something told him she'd walk away and wouldn't call back later to say she changed her mind. And damn it, Alexa was his only candidate. One year of his life was nothing compared to the gift of a future to do what he always dreamed about.

He gave her credit. She didn't even gloat.

She turned back around and spoke in a crisp, businesslike tone. "I know the contract doesn't state our new agreement. Do you give me your word you'll stick to the terms?"

"I can draw up a revised document."

"No need. Do you give me your word?"

Her figure shimmered with energy. Nick realized she trusted him on the same level he trusted her. A prickle of satisfaction ran through him. "I give you my word."

"Then I'll shake on it. Oh, and the dissolution of the marriage after one year? My family can't be hurt in this deception. We cite irreconcilable differences and pretend to part friends."

"I can live with that."

"Good. Pick me up tonight at seven and we'll go see my family to break the news. I'll take care of all the wedding arrangements."

He nodded, his brain a bit foggy from his decision and her nearness. Was that subtle fragrance from her skin vanilla? Or cinnamon? He watched in a daze while she dropped a business card on the cherrywood table.

"My address at the bookstore," she said. "I'll see you tonight."

He cleared his throat to reply, but it was too late. She had already left.

Chapter Three

Alexa squirmed in her seat as the silence in the black BMW stretched between them. Her husband-to-be seemed just as uncomfortable, and he chose to focus his energy into his MP3 player. She tried not to wince when he finally settled on Mozart. He actually enjoyed music without words. She almost shuddered again when she thought of sharing the same residence with him.

For. An. Entire. Year.

"Do you have any Black Eyed Peas?"

He looked puzzled by the question. "To eat?"

She held back a groan. "I'll even settle for some of the old classics. Sinatra, Bennett, Martin."

He remained silent.

"Eagles? Beatles? Just yell if any of these names sound familiar."

His shoulders stiffened. "I know who they are. Would you prefer Beethoven?"

"Forget it."

They veered into silence with a piano background. Alexa knew they were both nervous as the miles to her parents' house shortened. Playing the loving couple wouldn't be easy when they couldn't even carry on a two-minute conversation. She decided to try again.

"Maggie says you have a fish."

That remark rewarded her with a chilling look. "Yes."

"What's his name?"

"Fish."

She blinked. "You didn't even give it a name?"

"Did I commit a crime?"

"Don't you know animals have feelings just like people?"

"I don't like animals," he said.

"Why? Are you afraid of them?"

"Of course not."

"You were afraid of that snake we found in the woods. Remember how you wouldn't get close, and you made some excuse to leave?"

The air in the car seemed to drop a few degrees. "I wasn't afraid; I just didn't care. I told you I don't like animals."

She gave a snort, then settled back to silence. Cross another quality from her list. Earth Mother sucked. Alexa decided not to tell her future husband about the humane animal shelters. When they were overbooked, she always took the extra animals into her house until new spots opened up.

Something told her Nick would have a fit. If he ever got up enough emotion to lose control.

The possibility intrigued her.

"What are you smiling about?" he asked.

"Nothing. Do you remember everything we discussed?"

He gave a suffering sigh. "Yes. We went over all your family members in detail. I know names and general backgrounds. For God's sake, Alexa, I used to play at your house when we were younger."

She snorted. "You only wanted my mother's chocolate chip cookies. And you loved torturing your sister and me. Besides, that was years ago. You've had nothing to do with them over the past decade." She tried hard to bite back the bitterness, but the ease with which Nick had shed his past without a glance back left her a bit pissed off. "Speaking of which, you never mention your parents. Have you seen your father lately?"

She wondered if it were possible to get frostbite from the chill he emanated. "No."

She waited for more but nothing came. "How about your mom? Did she remarry?"

"No. I don't want to talk about my parents. There's no point."

"Wonderful. What are we supposed to tell my family about them? They'll ask."

His words were clipped. "Tell them my father's lounging in Mexico and my mother is off somewhere with her new boyfriend. Tell them whatever you want. They won't be at the wedding anyway."

She opened her mouth but his warning glare told her this conversation was over. Great. She just adored his chattiness.

Alexa pointed toward the upcoming street sign. "Here's the turn for my parents."

Nick pulled into the circular driveway and cut the engine. They both studied the white Victorian house. Even from outside, the structure radiated friendly warmth from each classic pillar to the graceful wraparound porch. Weeping willow trees surrounded the edges of the sloping lawn almost as in protection. Large picture windows with black shutters dotted the front. Darkness now veiled the symptoms of neglect due to financial difficulties. It hid the peeling white paint on the columns, the cracked step at the top of the patio, the worn roof. She gave a deep sigh as the home of her childhood settled around her like a comforting blanket.

"Are we ready?" he asked.

She glanced at him. His face was shuttered, his eyes distant. He looked hip and casual in his khaki Dockers, white Calvin Klein T-shirt, and leather boat shoes. His sun-bleached hair was neatly tamed except for one stubborn curl over his brow. His chest filled out the shirt nicely. A little too nicely for her taste. Obviously, he lifted weights. She wondered if he had a washboard stomach, but the thought did bad things to her own tummy, so she pushed away the idea and concentrated on their immediate problem.

"You look like you stepped in a pile of dog doo."

His neutral expression slipped. The corner of his mouth kicked up an inch. "Hmmm, Maggie said you wrote poetry."

"We're supposed to be madly in love. If they suspect

otherwise, I can't marry you, and my mother would make my life a living hell. So put on a good **act**. Oh, and don't be afraid to touch me. I promise I don't have cooties."

"I'm not afraid to—"

His breath hissed as she reached out and brushed the errant curl away from his eyes. The silky feel of his hair as it slid through her fingers pleased her. The shocked expression on his face tempted her to continue the caress by sliding the back of her hand down his cheek with one slow motion. His skin felt both smooth and rough to the touch.

"See? No big deal."

His full lips tightened with what she figured was annoyance. Obviously, Nick Ryan looked at her not as a grown woman, but as more of an asexual human being. Like an amoeba.

She flung open the door and cut off his response. "Show time."

He muttered something under his breath and followed her.

They didn't have to worry about ringing the doorbell. Her family streamed out the door one by one, until the front porch overflowed with her screeching sisters and two appraising males. Alexa had already called ahead to warn them of her engagement. She'd come up with a story about seeing Nick on the sly, a whirlwind romance, and an impulsive engagement. She played up their past so her parents believed they had always been in touch over the years as friends.

Nick tried to huddle back but her sisters refused to

comply. Isabella and Genevieve launched themselves into his arms for a big hug, chattering at once.

"Congratulations!"

"Welcome to the family!"

"Izzy, I told you he'd turn out to be gorgeous. How awesome is this? Childhood friends and now husband and wife!"

"Did you set a wedding date?"

"Can I be in the bridal party?"

Nick looked as if he were about to vault over the porch and make his escape.

Alexa collapsed into laughter. She cut off her younger twin sisters by pulling them to her for a hug. "Stop scaring him, guys. I finally got a fiancé. Don't ruin this for me."

They giggled. A double vision of two sixteen-year-old girls with chocolate hair, navy eyes, and long skinny legs stood before her. One had braces, one didn't. Alexa bet their teachers were grateful for the distinction. Her sisters were full of mischief and loved playing the switch game.

A demanding squeal pulled her attention away. She lifted up the blond angel at her feet and covered her three-year-old niece with kisses. "Taylor the Troublemaker," she said, "meet Nick Ryan. Uncle Nick to you, squirt."

Taylor looked him over with the careful attentive-ness only a child exudes. Nick awaited her opinion with patience. Then her face broke into a sunny smile. "Hi, Nick!"

He smiled back. "Hi, Taylor."

"Approval bestowed," Alexa said. She urged Nick over. "Let me make the rest of the introductions. My twin sisters, Isabella and Genevieve, now all grown up and out of diapers."

She ignored their dual groans and grinned. "My sister-in-law, Gina, and you know my brother, Lance, and my parents. Everyone, this is Nick Ryan, my fiancé."

She didn't even stumble over the word.

Her mother grabbed Nick's cheeks and gave him a smacking kiss. "Nicky, you're all grown up." She flung out her arms in welcome. "And you're so handsome."

Alexa wondered if that were a hint of red on Nick's cheeks, then dismissed the thought.

He cleared his throat. "Umm, thank you, Mrs. McKenzie. It's been a long time."

Lance gave him a friendly punch in the shoulder. "Hey, Nick, haven't seen you in centuries. Now I hear you're going to be part of the family. Congrats."

"Thanks."

Her father walked over and stuck out his hand. "Call me Jim," he said. "I remember you used to torture my little girl on many occasions. I think her first official curse word came out with you in mind."

"I think I still have that effect," Nick said wryly.

Her father laughed. Gina broke out of Lance's embrace to give him a big hug. "Now maybe I'll have someone to even out the odds around here," she said. Her green eyes sparkled. "You can get outnumbered in family meetings."

Alexa laughed. "He's still a man, Gina. Trust me, he'll take Lance's side every time."

Lance grabbed his wife back and wrapped his arms around her waist. "The odds are turning, baby. I finally got another man in the house to battle all the PMS."

Alexa punched his arm. Gina punched the other one.

Maria clucked her tongue. "Lancelot, men do not speak like that with ladies around."

"What ladies?"

Maria swatted him on the backside. "Everyone inside. We'll have a champagne toast, eat, and then have some good espresso."

"Can I have champagne?"

"Me, too?"

Maria shook her head at the two girls begging at her feet. "You'll have sparkling apple cider. I bought a bottle for this occasion."

"Me, too! Me, too!"

Alexa smiled down at the shiny-eyed toddler in her arms. "Okay, squirt. Apple juice for you, too." She placed her niece back on the ground and watched her race to the kitchen to get in on all the excitement. The embracing warmth of her clan settled around her like a fuzzy cloak and fought with the nerves jumping in her belly.

Could she pull this off? Casting a love spell to meet a nameless, faceless man with money to bail out her family was one thing. Nick Ryan in the flesh for one full year was another. If her parents suspected she had made a marriage bargain to save the house, they'd never forgive her. Or themselves. With the steady stream of medical bills from her father's heart condition, family pride pushed them to refuse any financial help from others. Knowing their daughter sacrificed her integrity to bail them out would break their hearts.

Nick watched her with a strange expression on his face, as

if trying to figure something out. Her fingers clenched to keep from reaching out to touch him. "You okay?" she asked.

"I'm fine. Let's go in."

She watched him walk inside and tried not to feel hurt by his clipped words. He'd already warned her he didn't like big families. She shouldn't be childish by taking his actions so personally.

She stiffened her resolve and her chin and followed him. The hours passed with hearty Italian lasagna, fresh garlic bread with cheese and herbs, and a bottle of Chianti. By the time they retired to the living room for espresso and Sambuca, a nice buzz hummed in her blood, fueled by good food and good conversation. She glanced up at Nick as he settled himself next to her at a careful distance on the worn beige sofa.

Misery etched his features.

He listened politely, laughed in the right places, and did a perfect job of looking like a gentleman. Except he wouldn't look her in the eye, moved away when she tried to touch him, and wasn't acting at all like the besotted fiancé he was supposed to be.

Jim McKenzie sipped his espresso with a casual demeanor. "So, Nick, tell me about your job."

"Dad—"

"No, it's okay." Nick turned to face her father. "Dreamscape is an architectural firm that designs buildings in the Hudson Valley. We designed the Japanese restaurant at the top of the mountain in Suffern."

Her father's face lit up. "Wonderful place to eat. Maria

always loved the gardens there." He paused. "So, what do you think of Alexa's paintings?"

She hid a wince. Oh, God, this was bad. Very bad. Her painting was a futile attempt at artistic expression, and most agreed they sucked. She painted more for her own therapy than to wow others. She cursed herself for not letting him pick her up at the apartment instead of her bookstore. As an alcoholic counselor, Jim honed in on weaknesses like a trained vulture and now he scented blood.

Nick kept the smile pasted on. "They're fantastic. I've always told her she should hang them in a gallery."

Jim crossed his arms. "You like them, huh? Which one do you like the most?"

"Dad—"

"The landscape one. Definitely puts you right at the scene."

Panic flirted with her slight drunken buzz as her father caught the tension between them and stalked him like a predator. She gave Nick credit for trying, but he had been doomed before he began. The rest of her family knew the drill and watched the process begin.

"She doesn't paint landscapes." The words hung in the air like a cannon blast.

Nick's smile never faltered. "She just tried her hand at landscapes. Darling, didn't you tell them?"

She fought back panic. "No, sorry, Dad, I haven't brought you up to speed. I'm painting mountain landscapes now."

"You hate landscapes."

"Not anymore," she managed cheerily. "I have a new

appreciation for landscapes since meeting an architect."

Her comment only elicited a snort before he continued. "So, Nick, baseball fan or football?"

"Both."

"Great season for the Giants, huh? I'm hoping for another New York Super Bowl. Hey, have you read Alexa's new poem?"

"Which one?"

"The one about the rainstorm."

"Oh, yes. I thought it was wonderful."

"She never wrote a poem about a rainstorm. She writes about experiences in life relating to love or loss. She's never written a nature poem, just as she's never painted a landscape."

Alexa chugged the rest of her Sambuca, ignored the espresso, and hoped the liquor got her through the evening. "Umm, Dad, I just wrote one about a rainstorm."

"Really? Would you recite it for us? Your mother and I haven't heard some of your new work."

She swallowed. "Well, it's still in creation mode. I'll definitely share as soon as it's perfect."

"But you let Nick see it."

Sickness clawed at her gut, and she prayed for escape. Her palms grew damp. "Yes. Well, Nick, maybe we better get going. It's late and I have a lot of wedding plans to get together."

Jim put his elbows on his knees. The circling stopped and he launched in for the kill. The rest of the family watched with impending doom. The sympathetic look on her brother's face told her he didn't think there'd be a wedding any longer. He wrapped his arms around his wife's waist as if reliving his own horror when he'd announced she was pregnant and they were getting married. Taylor busied herself with Legos and ignored the crisis.

"I meant to ask you about the wedding," Jim said. "You're putting it together in a week. Why not give everyone some time to get to know Nick and welcome him into the family? Why the rush?"

Nick tried to save them both. "I understand, Jim, but Alexa and I talked about this and we both don't want a big fuss. We decided we want to be together and start our lives right away."

"It's romantic, Dad," Izzy ventured.

Alexa mouthed a thank-you but she was suddenly double-teamed.

"I agree." Maria held a dishtowel in her hands as she stood in the doorway of the kitchen. "Let us enjoy the wedding. We'd love to throw you an engagement party so Nick can meet the rest of the family. There's just not time for everyone to come down on Saturday. All your cousins will miss out."

Jim stood. "Then it's settled. You'll postpone the date."

Maria nodded. "Excellent idea."

Alexa grabbed Nick's hand. "Darling, can I see you in the bedroom for a second?"

"Of course, dear."

She dragged him down the hallway and pushed him into the bedroom. The door swung partially closed. "You've ruined everything," she whispered furiously. "I told you to pretend but you suck at it and now my parents know we're not in love!"

"*I* suck at it? You're acting like this is some stupid play you've put together for the neighbors. This is real life, and I'm doing the best I can."

"My plays were not stupid. We made a lot of money in admission tickets. I thought *Annie* was excellent."

He snorted. "You can't even sing and you cast yourself as Annie."

"You're still pissed because I wouldn't let you play Daddy Warbucks."

He plowed ten fingers through his hair and made a noise deep in his throat. "How the hell do you get me on these ridiculous subjects?"

"You better come up with something quick. God, don't you know how to treat a girlfriend? You acted like I was some polite stranger. No wonder my father suspects!"

"You're a grown-up now, Alexa, and he's still interrogating your boyfriends. We don't need their permission. We get married on Saturday, and if your parents don't like it, too bad."

"I want my father to walk me down the aisle!"

"It's not even a real wedding!"

"It's the best I'm going to get right now!" The grief leaked out for one moment as the truth of her predicament hit full force. This would never be a real marriage, and something would be forever ruined once Nick's ring slipped onto her finger. She'd always dreamed of love everlasting, white picket fences, and tons of children. Instead, she got cold hard cash and a husband who politely tolerated her. She'd be damned if her sacrifice failed because of his inability to fake enough emotion for her parents.

She stood on tiptoe and grabbed the upper arms of his

T-shirt. Her nails dug into the fabric and cut flesh. "You better fix this," she hissed.

"What do you want me to do?"

She blinked. Her lip trembled as she bit out the words. "Do *something*, damn it! Prove to my father this will be a real marriage or—"

"Alexa?" The echo of her name drifted into the open door from the hallway, her mother's gentle, concerned voice checking if they were okay.

"Your mother's coming," he said.

"I know—she probably heard us arguing. Do something!"

"What?"

"Anything!"

"Fine!" He grabbed her around the waist, dragged her body flush against his, and ducked his head. His lips crushed hers as his hands wrapped around her tightly so they were plastered against each other, hip to hip, thigh to thigh, breasts to chest.

The breath whooshed out of her lungs and she swayed as her feet cut out on her. She expected a precise, controlled kiss to calmly show her mother they were lovers. Instead she got hot testosterone and raw sexual energy. She got warm lips melded over hers. His teeth nipped. His tongue burrowed inside and plunged in and out with sheer command, bending her back over his arm to take every last drop of her resolve.

She hung on and gave it all back. Ravenous for his touch, she got drunk on his musky scent and taste, reveled in the hard length of his body as animal heat rose between them and pushed them over the edge.

She moaned deep in her throat. He slid his fingers into the heavy weight of her hair to hold her head still as he continued the sensual invasion. Her breasts grew heavy and full, and liquid heat pulsed between her thighs.

"Alexa, I—oh!"

Nick ripped his mouth from hers. Dazed, Alexa searched his face for some sign of emotion, but he focused on her mother. "I'm sorry, Maria." His grin was wry and totally male.

Maria laughed and looked at her daughter, still snug in his arms. "Sorry to interrupt. Come join us when you're finished."

Alexa heard footsteps retreating. Slowly, Nick's gaze traveled downward.

She shuddered. She expected to see a fog of passion. Instead, his chestnut eyes were clear. His face seemed calm. If not for the hard length pressed against her thigh, Alexa would have thought the kiss hadn't affected him. She was dragged back to another time and place, deep in the woods, when her thoughts had been freely spoken and her trust shattered. The first touch of his lips over hers, the boyish scent of cologne rising to her nostrils, the gentle bite of his fingers on her hips as he held her.

Icy fear trickled down her spine. If he laughed at her again, she'd call off the whole thing. If he laughed…

His arms released her and he stepped back. Silence surged between them like a heavy wave gaining speed and ready to crash.

"I think we solved our problem," he said.

She didn't respond.

"Isn't this what you wanted?"

She stuck her chin high in the air and hid the messy emotions that writhed like snakes in her belly. "I guess so."

He paused, then reached for her. "We better present a united front."

Five fingers closed around hers with a graceful strength that brought tears to her eyes. She fought them back and decided she was in major PMS mode. There was no other reason why a kiss from Nick Ryan should bring so much pleasure, yet hurt so deeply.

"Are you okay?"

She gritted her teeth and smiled so brightly she could have done an advertisement for toothpaste. "Of course. Brilliant idea, by the way."

"Thank you."

"Just don't stiffen up again like a corpse out there. Pretend I'm Gabriella."

"I could never confuse you and Gabriella."

The cutting remark slashed through her but she refused to show weakness. "I'm sure you're right. But you're no fantasy for me, either, Pretty Boy."

"I didn't mean—"

"Forget it." She led him back out into the living room. "Sorry for the interruption, guys. I think we better get going; it's late."

Everyone jumped up to say good-bye. Maria kissed her cheek and winked with approval. "I may not like the rush," she whispered, "but you're a grown woman. Ignore your father and follow your heart."

Her throat tightened. "Thanks, Mom. We've got a lot to do this week."

"Don't worry, honey."

They were almost to the door when Jim made a last-ditch attempt. "Alexandria, the least you could do is postpone the wedding a few weeks for the family. Nick, surely you can't disagree?"

Nick put his hand on her father's shoulder. His other firmly clasped his fiancée's. "I understand why you want us to wait, Jim. But you see, I'm madly in love with your daughter, and we're getting married on Saturday. We really want your blessing."

Everyone grew quiet. Even Taylor stopped her babbling to watch the scene before her. Alexa waited for the explosion.

Jim nodded. "Okay. Can I pull you aside for a moment?"

"Dad—"

"Just for a moment." Nick followed Jim into the kitchen.

Alexa bit back the worry as she chatted with Izzy and Gen about bridesmaid dresses. She caught a glimpse of Nick's serious expression as he listened to her father. After a few minutes, they shook hands and Jim looked a bit chastened as he kissed her good-bye.

They said their final farewells and got into the car. "What did my father want?"

Nick pulled out of the driveway and concentrated on the road in front of him. "He was worried about paying for the wedding."

Guilt assaulted her in massive gulps. She'd completely forgotten about the wedding expenses. Of course, her father probably assumed he'd pay, even though times had changed. Sweat pricked her forehead. "What did you tell him?"

Nick glanced at her. "I refused to let him pay and told him if I'd done what he asked and waited a year, I'd accept his money. But because this was our decision to rush the wedding, I insisted I foot the bill. So we made a bargain. He pays for his tux and your brother's. I pay for all the girls' dresses—including yours—and the rest of the wedding."

She let out her breath in a rush and studied him in the flash of oncoming headlights. His face remained expressionless, but his gesture tugged at her heart. "Thank you," she said softly.

He jerked as if her words punched through him. "No need. I'd never hurt your parents. No one usually has enough money to pay for a wedding in a week. And I understand family pride. I'd never strip them of that."

She choked back emotion as they drove for a while in silence. Alexa stared out the window into the darkness. His offer suggested a real relationship between them, and it made her long for more. She should have introduced her family to a real-life love—not a fake. The lies of the night pressed down on her spirits as she realized she'd made a bargain with the devil for cold hard cash. Cash to save her family. But cash nonetheless.

His gravelly voice broke the silence and her gloomy thoughts. "You seemed upset about our little ruse tonight."

"I hate lying to my family."

"Then why do it?"

An uncomfortable silence settled between them.

Nick pressed on. "How badly do you want this money? You don't seem too thrilled with the idea of marrying me. You're lying to your family and holding a fake wedding. All for a business expansion? You could get a loan from a bank like most businesses do. Something isn't adding up."

The words bubbled up and she almost told him the truth. Her father's sickness shortly after his return. The lack of medical insurance to pay the staggering bills. Her brother's struggle to get through medical school while supporting a new family. The endless calls from collectors until her mother had no choice but to sell the house, already heavily mortgaged.

And the weight of responsibility and helplessness Alexa carried along the way.

"I need the money," she said simply.

"Need? Or want?"

She closed her eyes at the taunt. He wanted to believe she was selfish and shallow. In that moment, she realized she needed every defense against this man. His kiss had shattered all illusions of neutrality between them. His lips over hers had rocked her to the bottom of her soul, just like the very first time in the woods. Nicholas Ryan tore through her walls and left her vulnerable. After a week living in close quarters, she'd be jumping his bones.

Alexa had no other choice.

She needed to cultivate his hatred for her. If he thought she was a shady character, he'd leave her alone and she'd walk away with her pride intact and her family whole. She refused to foster his pity or take his charity. If she told the truth about her family, the rest of her defenses would shatter. He may even give her the money free and clear, and then she'd be forever in his debt.

The image of him casting her in a role of the martyr to

save Tara choked her with humiliation. No, better off that he believe her to be a coldhearted businesswoman as he craved. At least he'd resent her and keep his distance. Just being near the man set her off like a firecracker, and she'd be damned if she took a backseat to his precious Gabriella.

Her deal with the devil would be on her own terms.

Alexa drew on her inner reserve and lapsed into her second phase of lies for the night. "You really want to know the truth?"

"Yeah. I want to know."

"You grew up with money, Pretty Boy. Money smooths out a lot of unhappiness and stress. I'm tired of struggling like my mother. I don't want to wait another five years before expanding my bookstore. I don't want to deal with interest and banks and debt-to-income ratios. I'm going to use the money to build a café onto BookCrazy and make it a success."

"What if it fails? You'll be back where you started."

"The property is building in value, so I can always sell. And I'm putting the extra into a solid financial portfolio. I can buy a small house outright and be secure by the time our marriage dissolves."

"Why not ask for two hundred thousand? Or even more? Why not squeeze me dry?"

She shrugged. "I estimated one-fifty would be enough to give me everything I want. If I thought you'd give me more money, I would've asked. After all, other than dealing with my family, it's a pretty easy bargain. I just have to put up with you."

"I guess you're more logical than I thought." The statement should have been a compliment. She burned with humiliation but knew she'd bought the distance desperately needed. Of course, the price was her character. But she reminded herself of the goal and remained silent.

He pulled up to her apartment building. She opened the car door and grabbed her purse. "I'd invite you up, but I think we'll be seeing enough of each other in the next year."

He nodded. "Good night. I'll be in touch. I can have the movers help you whenever you're ready. Do whatever you want with the wedding and let me know where and when to show up."

"Okay. See ya."

"See ya."

She let herself into her apartment, closed the door behind her, and slid her back down the frame until she hit the floor.

Then cried.

. . .

Nick watched her safely enter her loft and waited for the light to click on. The low purr of the BMW was the only sound to break the silence.

His annoyance at her blunt admission bothered him. What did he care why she wanted the money? It was a perfect motivation to get them both through the next year with no damage. He needed to keep his distance. Her parents had caused a dangerous longing to bubble up from deep inside. He'd quickly squashed the emotion, but the idea that he still retained some sick ray of hope for a normal family pissed him off.

Maybe it was the way she looked tonight. She smiled so easily, her lips full and relaxed.

He'd wanted to dip his head and taste what lay beneath those ruby, bee-stung lips. Wanted to slip his tongue deep inside and tempt her to play. The snug material of her jeans showed off the curve of her buttocks and swing of her hips. A hot pink button-down shirt seemed conservative enough, until she leaned forward and Nick caught a glimpse of pale rose lace cupping her full breasts. The image burned through his mind and wreaked havoc with his concentration. He'd spent most of the evening trying to get her to bend down so he could sneak a peek. Just like a horny teenager.

The lightbulb kicked on and he roared away from the curb. Temper bit at him like a moody pit bull. She bothered him in a deep, gutted way. So did her family. He remembered how loving her mother had been. Remembered the guilt when he'd wished his own mother would disappear and leave him with Maria McKenzie. Remembered the old pain of being out of control in a world not meant for children to be alone in. Remembered things he'd vowed to never unearth. Marriage. Children. Connections only caused a ripping pain no one deserved.

He had erected walls so Alexa wouldn't spot any moments of weakness. If she suspected he desired her in any way, the rules would change. He hadn't intended for this siren of a woman to have any power over him.

Until the kiss.

Nick muttered a foul curse. He remembered how her breath came in choppy gasps and her eyes snapped. That damn shirt finally gaped open enough for him to spot ripe flesh encased in pink lace. He'd been ready to push her away, and then she'd grabbed him at her mother's call. Wasn't his fault he gave in to instinct to save their ruse.

Until her hot, wet mouth had opened under his. Until her sweet taste swamped his senses, and the maddening scents of vanilla and spice made him wild—no prisoners taken. Demanding. Punishing. Passionate.

He was so screwed. And not in a good way.

But she'd never know. He had made sure to screen his face to a nothing blankness, though his jutting erection screamed he was a liar. Didn't matter. Nick refused to break the rules. Alexa was a woman who lived in the light and would never be happy with the deal he'd made himself when he was a child. One year was enough.

He hoped he emerged in one piece.

Chapter Four

Nick turned to look at his sleeping bride. Her head rested against the door of the limousine. Her headpiece had been ripped off, and crumbled white lace lay at his feet. Raven curls shot off in all directions and hid her bare shoulders from view. The glass of champagne in the cup holder lay untouched, the bubbles gone flat. A sparkling two-carat diamond bound her finger and exploded sparks of light from the last rays of the dying sun. Plump, ruby lips parted to allow breath in and out. A delicate snore steadily rose in the air during each exhalation.

Alexandria Maria McKenzie was now his wife.

Nick reached for his own champagne glass and silently toasted to success. He now fully owned Dreamscape Enterprises. He was about to go after the opportunity of a lifetime and he didn't need anyone's permission. The day had gone off without a hitch.

He took a healthy swig of Dom Pérignon and wondered why he felt like crap. His mind flashed back to the moment the priest made them man and wife. Sapphire eyes filled with pure fear and panic as he leaned down to give her the necessary kiss. Pale and shaken, her lips trembled under his. He knew it wasn't with passion. At least not this time.

He reminded himself she only wanted the money. Her ability to pretend she was an innocent was dangerous. He mocked his own thoughts by raising his glass again and downing the last of the champagne.

The limo driver lowered the smoked window by a degree. "Sir, we've arrived at our destination."

"Thank you. You can pull up front."

As the limo climbed the long, narrow drive, Nick gently shook his bride awake. She stirred, snorted, and collapsed back into sleep. Nick fought a smile and started to whisper. Then stopped. He slipped back into his old role as tormentor with comfortable ease—he leaned over and yelled her name.

She shot straight up. Eyes wide with shock, she pushed her hair out of her ears and looked down at all the white lace like she was Alice in Wonderland down the rabbit hole. "Oh my God, we did it."

He handed over her shoes and headpiece. "Not yet, but it is our honeymoon. I'll be happy to oblige if you're in the mood."

She glared at him. "You didn't do anything for this wedding but show up. Try scheduling every last detail within seven days and I'll sit back and watch you collapse."

"I told you to get a justice of the peace."

Alexa snorted. "Typical male. You don't lift a finger to help and cry innocent when challenged."

"You snore."

Her mouth gaped. "I do not snore!"

"Do, too."

"Do not. Someone would have told me."

"I'm sure your lovers didn't want to be kicked out of bed. You're cranky."

"Am not."

"Are, too."

The door swung open and the chauffeur offered his arm to help her. She stuck out her tongue and left the limo with the haughtiness of Queen Elizabeth. He smothered another laugh and followed. Alexa stopped short at the curb. He watched her take in the arching lines of the mansion, which resembled a Tuscan villa. Sandstone terra-cotta created an image of casual elegance, and its high walls and large windows lent an aura of history. A lush green lawn hugged the drive and led up to the house, then sprawled out for acres in cheery abandon. Colorful geraniums spilled from each window box to mimic old-age Italy. The top of the house opened up to a wrought-iron balcony that held tables, chairs, and a hot tub sunk amidst leafy trees. She opened her mouth as if to comment, then shut it with a snap.

"What do you think?" he asked.

She tilted her head. "It's stunning," she said. "The most beautiful house I've ever seen."

Pleasure shot through him at her obvious delight. "Thank you. I designed it myself."

"It looks old."

"That was my goal. I promise I have all the necessary indoor plumbing."

She shook her head and followed him inside. Marble floors shone to high polish and cathedral ceilings created an illusion of space and elegance. Large, airy rooms set off the center spiral staircase. Nick tipped the driver and closed the door behind him. "Come on, I'll show you around. Unless you want to get undressed first."

She grabbed handfuls of gauzy material and lifted her train. Her stockinged feet peeked out from underneath. "Lead on."

He took her on the grand tour. The fully-equipped kitchen boasted a gleaming center of stainless steel and chrome, but Nick had made sure the room retained the warmth an Italian grandmother would be proud of. A heavily cut wooden island held baskets filled with fresh fruit and cloves of garlic, herbs sunk in bottles brimming with olive oil, dry pastas, and ripe red tomatoes. The table was thick oak with sturdy, comfortable chairs. An array of wines peeked out from an extensive wrought-iron rack. Glass doors led from the kitchen to the sunroom, complete with wicker furniture, bookcases, and vases of daisies spilling through the room. Instead of colorful paintings, black-and-white photographs took up wall space and displayed an array of architecture from around the world. Nick enjoyed her expressions as she took in every inch of his space. He led her up the staircase to the bedrooms.

"My room is down the hallway. I have a private office but there's a spare computer in the library you can use. I can order anything else you need." He pushed open one of the doors. "I've given you a room with a private bath. I wasn't sure of your taste, so feel free to redecorate."

He watched her take in the neutral, pale tones of the king-size poster bed and matching furniture.

"This will be fine. Thank you," she said.

He stared at her for a moment as the formality pulsed between them. "You know we're stuck here for at least two days, right? We used work as an excuse not to go on a honeymoon, but I can't show up at the office until Monday. People will gossip."

She nodded. "I can use the computer to keep up. And Maggie said she'd help out."

He turned. "Get comfortable and meet me down in the kitchen. I'll cook something for dinner."

"You cook?"

"I don't like strange people in my kitchen—I had enough of that growing up. So, I learned."

"Are you good?"

He snorted. "I'm the best."

Then he shut the door behind him.

. . .

Arrogant man.

Alexa turned and studied her new room. She knew Nick was comfortable living with grand wealth, but the tour had made her feel like Audrey Hepburn's character in *My Fair Lady*—hopelessly common beside the sophistication of her tutor.

The heck with it. She needed to keep her life as normal as possible, marriage or not. Nick was not her real husband, and she didn't intend to get sucked into any domestic ruse and find herself lost at the end of the year. She probably wouldn't even see him often. She assumed he also worked late hours, and besides the occasional party they'd need to attend, they'd lead separate lives.

Her mental pep talk helped, so she ripped off her dress and spent the next hour in a bubble bath in the luxurious spa tub in the bathroom attached to her room. She glanced just once at the sheer black nightie her sisters had thrown in her overnight bag, then shoved it to the back of a drawer. She threw on a pair of leggings and a cropped fleece sweatshirt, clipped up her hair, and made her way down to the kitchen. Alexa followed the sounds of crackling and slipped into one of the heavy carved chairs in the kitchen. She drew her bare feet up to the edge of her seat, wrapped her arms around her knees, and watched her new husband.

He hadn't changed out of his tuxedo. He'd taken off his jacket and had rolled the crisp white shirtsleeves up past his elbows. The onyx pearl buttons had been undone to mid-chest, and they revealed a mat of golden hair sprinkled across carved muscles. Alexa had a hell of a time ignoring the hard curve of his butt. The man had a great ass. Too bad she'd never see it naked. She didn't think seeing his bathing suit pulled down as a teenager counted. Besides, she'd been too busy staring at his front.

"Want to help?"

She dug her nails into her palm to give herself a reality boost. "Sure. What are we having?"

"Fettuccine Alfredo with shrimp, garlic bread, and a salad."

A distressed moan escaped her lips. "Oh God, you're mean."

"You don't like the menu?"

"I like it too much. I'll just have the salad."

He shot her a disgusted look over his shoulder. "I'm tired of females who order a salad, then look as if they deserve a medal. A good meal is a gift."

She clenched her fingers harder. "Well, thanks so much for that smug viewpoint of the female population. For your information, I can appreciate good food better than you. Did you see the appetizers I ordered for our wedding? Didn't you see how much I ate? Dammit, it's just like a man to put a rich, fattening meal in front of a woman and get offended when she won't eat. Then you seem shocked in the bedroom when you're looking at her hips and wondering how she put on ten extra pounds!"

"Nothing wrong with curves on a woman."

She bolted out of her chair and grabbed the ingredients for salad. "I've heard that one before. Let's put this to the test, shall we? How much does Gabriella weigh?"

He didn't answer.

She threw a red pepper on the table next to the romaine lettuce and snorted. "Oh, are we tongue-tied now? Is she one hundred pounds or is that considered fat nowadays?"

When he spoke, his tone was less cocky. "She's a model. She has to retain a lighter weight."

"And does she order salads when she goes out to dinner?"

More silence.

A cucumber rolled over the counter and stopped at the edge. "Ah, I guess that means yes. But I'm sure you appreciate her discipline when you rip her clothes off."

He shifted his feet and kept his attention on the pan sizzling with shrimp. "Gabriella is a bad example." He definitely sounded uncomfortable.

"I have another puzzle. Maggie said you tend to date only models. Seems you like skinny women and accept them eating a salad." She rinsed the vegetables, grabbed a knife, and started hacking. "But if it's someone you're not thinking of sleeping with, I guess you don't care how fat she gets as long as she keeps you company at meals."

"I happen to detest going out to dinner with most of my dates. I understand they're in the business, but I enjoy a woman who likes good food and isn't afraid to eat it. You're not fat. You never were fat, so I don't know where this obsession comes from."

"You called me fat once."

"I did not."

"Yes, you did. When I was fourteen, you told me I was filling out in all the wrong places."

"Hell, woman, I meant your breasts. I was a snotty teenager who wanted to torture you. You were always beautiful."

Silence descended.

She looked up from her task and her mouth gaped open. In all the years she'd known Nick Ryan, he had teased, tortured, and insulted her.

He had never called her beautiful.

Nick whisked the cream, his tone casual. "You know what I mean. Beautiful in the sense of sisterly. I watched you and Maggie go through puberty and grow into women. Neither of you are ugly. Or fat. I think you're being hard on yourself."

Alexa understood what he meant. He didn't think of her as a beautiful woman, more like as an annoying younger sister who grew up to be attractive. The difference was monumental, and she ignored the sharp sting of hurt. "Well, I'm going to eat this salad and I don't want to hear any more comments about women."

"Fine. Would you open a bottle of wine? There's one chilling in the fridge."

She uncorked an expensive chardonnay and watched him sip it. The citrusy scents of wood and fruit rose to her nostrils. She battled for one minute, then surrendered. One glass. After all, she deserved it.

She poured herself a glass and took a sip. The liquid slid down the back of her throat, the taste both tingly and dry. She uttered a low moan of pleasure. Her tongue licked the edges of her lips and her eyes closed as the flavor pulsed through her body.

. . .

Nick started to say something, then stopped cold. The sight of her sipping and enjoying her wine put every muscle in his body in a lock. The blood pounded through his veins and his groin shot to full alert. Her tongue licked her lips with such delicate strokes, he wished she tasted something other than the wine.

He wondered if she made those throaty sounds when a man was buried deep inside her wet, clinging heat. He wondered if she'd be as tight and hot as her mouth, closing around him like a silky fist, milking every last drop of his reserve and still demanding more. Those stretchy pants revealed every curve of her body, from her sweet butt to the luscious length of her legs. Her sweatshirt had ridden up and flashed him with a strip of bare skin. And obviously she'd ripped off her bra, not thinking of him as a man who wanted her, but more like an annoying older brother without male urges.

Damn her for starting to make things complicated. He dropped the bowl of pasta on the table and quickly arranged the place settings.

"Stop drinking the wine like that. You're not in a porno flick."

She gasped. "Hey, don't take things out on me just 'cause you're cranky. I can't help it if business was more important to you than a real marriage."

"Yeah, but as soon as I gave a price, you jumped. I bought you just as much as you bought me."

She grabbed the pasta bowl and filled her plate. "Who are you to judge me? You've had everything given to you your whole life. You got a Mitsubishi Eclipse for your sixteenth birthday. I got a Chevette."

He stiffened at the memory. "You got a family. I got shit."

She paused, then grabbed a piece of hot garlic bread dripping with mozzarella. "You got Maggie."

"I know."

"What happened to you guys? You used to be close."

He shrugged. "She changed in high school. Suddenly, she wouldn't talk to me. She stopped letting me in her room for our talks, then shut me out completely. So, I let her go and concentrated on having a life of my own. You lost touch with her for a while back then, didn't you?"

"Yeah. I always thought something happened, but she never talks about it. Anyway, my own family was screwed up for a while, so you weren't alone."

"But now it's like *The Waltons* in there."

She laughed and crammed a mouthful of pasta into her mouth. "My father has a lot to make up for, but I think we've managed to heal the cycle."

"Cycle?"

"The karmic cycle, when someone screws up really badly and hurts you. Our first instinct is to hurt back or refuse to forgive."

"Sounds reasonable."

"Ah, but now the cycle of hurt and abuse continues. When he came back, I decided I only had one father, and I'd accept whatever he could give. Eventually, he gave up the booze and tried to make up for the past."

Nick made a rude sound. "He took off when you were young and left his family behind for the bottle. Abandoned your twin sisters. Then he shows up asking for forgiveness? Why would you even want him in your life?"

She forked another shrimp and let it hover right before her lips. "I made a choice," she said. "I'll never forget, but if my own mother learned to forgive him, how can I refuse? Family sticks together no matter what happens."

The simplicity of her ability to forgive shook him to the core. He poured more wine. "Better to walk away with your head held high and your pride intact. Let them suffer for all the pain they caused."

She seemed to think his words over. "I almost did. But I realized besides being my father, he's just a human being who screwed up. I'd have my pride, but I wouldn't have a father. When I made my decision I broke the cycle. He ended up getting sober and rebuilt our relationship. Have you ever thought of contacting your father?"

His emotions slammed into hyper-speed. Nick fought past the old bitterness and managed a shrug. "Jed Ryan doesn't exist in my eyes. That was my decision." He prepared for pity but her face only reflected a deep empathy that soothed him. How many times had he craved an actual beating or a punishment from his father instead of neglect? Somehow, the not caring burned deeper and festered.

"What about your mom?"

He concentrated on his plate. "She's shacked up with another actor. She likes when they're in show business. It makes her feel important."

"Do you see her often?"

"The idea of an adult son reminds her of her age. She likes to pretend I don't exist."

"I'm sorry."

The words were simple but straight from the heart. Nick looked up from his plate. For one second, awareness and energy and understanding pulsed in the air between them, then slid away as if it had never occurred. His lopsided smile mocked his own confession. "Poor little rich boy. But you're right about one thing—that was a hell of a Mitsubishi."

She laughed and changed the subject. "Tell me about the deal you're working on. Must be something big in order to remain celibate for a year."

He let the smart-mouthed comment slide but shot her a warning look. "I want to involve Dreamscape in a bid to build down by the waterfront."

One brow arched. "I heard they want to build a spa, along with a few restaurants. Everyone's buzzing about it. People used to be afraid to go near the river."

He leaned forward with eagerness. "The area's changing. They've beefed up security, and the few bars and shops already there are doing well. This will break the area wide open to both residents and tourism. Can you picture lit pathways along the water with outside lounges? How about a huge spa that overlooks the mountains while you get a massage? It's the future."

"I also heard they only want the biggest companies in Manhattan to bid on the job."

His body clenched in an almost physical need. His dream was right before him and he'd let nothing stand in his way. He drilled out the words like a mantra. "I'm going to get that contract."

She blinked, then slowly nodded as if his own belief secured hers. "Can Dreamscape handle such a job?"

He took a sip of wine. "The board thinks it's too ambitious, but I'm going to prove them wrong. If I succeed, Dreamscape will rise to the top."

"Is it about the money?"

He shook his head. "I don't care about the money. I want to make my mark, and I know how I want to approach it. Nothing too citified. Nothing to compete with the mountains, but a structure that bows to nature and blends, rather than fighting back."

"It sounds like you've thought about this for a long time."

He sopped up the last piece of bread in the remaining sauce, then popped it into his mouth. "I knew the city would make this decision soon, and I wanted to be prepared. I've been thinking about designs by the river for years. Now I'm ready."

"How are you going to get it?"

Nick concentrated on his plate. Funny, she seemed able to tell when he lied. Had from childhood. "I already have one of the partners on board. Richard Drysell is building the spa, and we share the same vision. He's having a dinner party next Saturday. The final two men I need to convince will be there, so I'm hoping to make an impression." He didn't share how Alexa fit into the mix. He looked upon his new wife as a way to close the deal, but it would be better explained the night of the party.

Nick lifted his head and spotted her cleaned plate.

The full salad bowl remained on the table between them, untouched. The pasta and bread and wine were depleted. She looked like she was on the verge of exploding. "Well, the salad looks awfully good. Aren't you going to eat it?"

She forced a bright smile and forked up a leafy piece. "Of course. I adore salads."

He grinned. "Any dessert?"

She let out a groan. "Funny." They cleaned up quickly, stacked everything in the dishwasher, and then she stretched out on the camel-colored sofa in the living room. Nick figured she was hoping for a faster way to digest.

"Are you going to work tonight?" she asked.

"No, it's late. What about you?"

"Nah, too tired." The room filled with a short silence. "So, what do you want to do?"

Her shirt snaked up a precious inch. The smooth, tanned skin of her stomach wreaked havoc with his concentration. He had some very clear images of what they could do. They involved slowly lifting her shirt. Then licking her nipples until they tightened under his tongue. The rest centered on stripping off those sweatpants and testing how fast he could make her burn up in his arms. Since none of those options was possible, he gave a shrug. "Don't know. TV? Movie?"

She shook her head. "Poker."

"Excuse me?"

Her eyes lit up. "Poker. I have a deck of cards in my suitcase."

"You carry your own cards?"

"You never know when you'll need them."

"What do we play for?"

She jumped up from the sofa and headed toward the stairs. "Money, of course. Unless you're too chicken."

"Fine. But we'll use my cards."

She stopped mid-flight and looked at him. "Okay. I deal."

He hit the remote and strains of *Madame Butterfly* echoed

from the Bose speakers. He topped off their glasses and settled by the coffee table. She sat beside him, legs crossed. Her fingers flew through the cards with the ease of an expert, shuffling with lightning speed. Nick had a flash of her in a low-cut dress, dealing cards in a saloon while she sat on a cowboy's lap. He shook off the image and concentrated on his hand.

"Dealer's choice. Five-card stud. Ante up."

He frowned. "With what?" he asked.

"I told you we're playing for money."

"Should I have my butler unlock the safe? Or maybe we'll just play for the family jewels?"

"Very funny. Don't you have any singles laying around?"

His lip quirked. "Sorry. Only hundreds."

"Oh."

She seemed so disappointed he lost the battle and chuckled. "How about we play for something more interesting?"

"I don't play strip poker."

"I meant favors."

Her teeth caught her bottom lip. He watched the action with pure pleasure.

"What kind of favors?" she asked.

"The first one to win three full hands gets a free favor from the other. It can be used any time, like a voucher."

Her face lit up with interest. "You can use the favor toward anything? No rules?"

"No rules."

The challenge drew her in like a pure-blooded gambler on the scent of a long shot. He sensed his victory even before she agreed. Nick practically licked his lips as she consented, and he knew for the next few months he'd finally have the control he needed in this marriage.

She dealt. He almost laughed at the obvious outcome, but he refused to be merciful. She threw one card out and scooped up a replacement.

He laid down his cards. "Full house."

"Two jacks. Your deal."

Nick gave her credit—she refused to buckle. Kept her emotions firmly hidden. He bet her father taught her, and if not for Nick's past experience, she'd be a hell of a player to beat. She tossed down a pair of aces and surrendered gracefully to his three fours.

"One more hand," he said.

"I can count. My deal." Her fingers flew over the cards. "So, where'd you learn poker?"

He viewed his hand nonchalantly. "Buddy of mine kept a weekly game. It was a good excuse to do some serious drinking and hanging out."

"Always thought you were more the chess type."

He tossed in a card and replaced it. "I'm good at that, too."

She gave an unladylike snort. "Show." She displayed her straight and triumph gleamed in her eyes.

He almost felt sorry for her. Almost.

"Good hand." He offered her a cocky grin. "But not good enough." He threw down four aces. Then stretched his legs out in front of him and leaned back. "Nice try, though."

She gaped in astonishment at his cards. "The odds of four aces in five-card stud are… Oh my God, you cheated!"

He shook his head and made a *tsk*ing sound. "Come on,

Al, I thought you were a better competitor. Are you still a sore loser? Now about my favor…"

Nick wondered if actual steam leaked from her pores. "Nobody can get four aces unless he palmed the cards. Don't lie to me, because I was thinking of doing it myself!"

"Don't accuse me of something you can't prove."

"You cheated." Her tone held a twist of wonder-ment and horror. "You lied to me on our wedding night."

He snorted. "If you don't want to pay your debt, say so. Just like a woman to be a bad loser."

She squirmed with hot-blooded emotion. "You're a swindler, Nick Ryan."

"Prove it."

"I will."

She launched herself over the coffee table and into his arms. The breath whooshed out of him as she tumbled him back onto the carpet and stuck her hand up his shirtsleeves for the suspected planted cards. Nick grunted as a full female figure pressed flush against every muscle, intent only on finding evidence of foul play. He tried to push her off but she switched her attention to his shirt pockets and he laughed. The sound started deep in his chest and he realized this woman had made him laugh more in the past week than he had since childhood. When her fingers slipped into his pants pocket, he realized if she delved any deeper she wouldn't come up empty-handed. The laughter eased into a hard twist deep in his gut and with one quick motion he flipped her onto her back, laid on top of her, and pinned both hands beside her head.

Her hair clip had come out during the scuffle. Coal-black

curls tumbled over her face and covered one side. Snapping blue eyes peeked between the strands, filled with a haughty contempt only she could pull off after tackling him to the ground for a wrestling match. Her breasts rose against her fleece top, unbound. Her legs entwined with his, her thighs slightly parted.

Nick was in deep trouble.

"I know you have the cards planted. Just admit it and we'll forget this whole thing happened."

"You're crazy, you know," he muttered. "Don't you ever think about the consequences of your actions?"

She stuck her bottom lip out and blew a hard breath. The curls obediently slid away from her eyes. "I didn't cheat."

Her mouth pouted. He smothered a curse, and his fingers tightened around her wrists. Damn her for making him want. Damn her for not seeing it.

"We're not kids anymore, Alexa. Next time you go tackling a man to the ground, be prepared to take the heat."

"Who are you, Clint Eastwood? Is your next line going to be, 'Go ahead, make my day'?"

The heat in his groin rose to his head like a swarming fog, until he could only think about the wet heat of her mouth and the soft body beneath him. He wanted to be naked with her in a tangle of sheets, and instead she treated him like an annoying older brother. But that wasn't even the worst part. She was his wife. The thought tortured him. Some buried, caveman instinct flared to life and pushed him to make his claim. By law, she already belonged to him.

And tonight was their wedding night.

She challenged him to turn anger to desire, to feel her lips slick and trembling under his, all sweetness and surrender and passion. The normal logic of his list and his plan and his need for a business marriage flew out the window.

He decided to claim his wife.

• • •

Alexa felt the man on top of her hold his body in a tight muscle lock. She'd been so intent on their argument, she'd forgotten he pinned her to the carpet. She opened her mouth to make another smart remark about bondage, then stopped. Met his eyes. And sucked in her breath.

Oh, God.

Primitive sexual energy swirled between them like a tornado gaining speed and power. His eyes burned with a sheen of fire, half need, half anger as he stared down at her. She realized he lay between her open thighs, his hips angled over hers, his chest propped up as he gripped at her fingers. This was no longer the teasing indulgence of a brother. This was no old friend or business partner. This was the simple want of a man to a woman, and Alexa felt herself dragged down into the storm with her body's own cry.

"Nick?"

Her voice was raspy. Hesitant. Her nipples pushed against the soft fleece with demand. His gaze raked over her face, her breasts, her exposed stomach. The tension pulled taut between them. He lowered his head. The rush of his breath caressed her lips as he spoke right against her mouth.

"This means nothing."

His body contradicted his words as he claimed her mouth in a fierce kiss. With one quick thrust, his tongue pushed through the seam of her lips to travel beyond. Her mind fogged, caught between the dull pain of his statement and the pleasure pounding through her in waves. She gripped his hands and hung on, reveling in the dark taste of hunger and expensive chardonnay, rocking her hips upward to meet the hard length of his body and rubbing her nipples against his chest. She lost control in those few moments, the ageless empty void of the past years temporarily filled with the taste and feel and smell of him.

Her tongue matched every thrust as a low guttural groan escaped her throat. He ripped his fingers away from hers and slid his palms up over her belly and cupped her breasts. Her nipples tightened, and he pushed the cloth up higher. He stared at her naked breasts, and the heat in his eyes nearly burned her alive. One thumb tweaked her nipple and she cried out. His head lowered. Alexa realized this was the moment of truth. If he kissed her again, she'd surrender. Her body ached for his and she couldn't come up with one damn good reason to stop.

The doorbell rang.

The sound ricocheted off the walls. Nick jerked upward and rolled off her like a politician caught in the middle of a sex scandal, muttering some nasty words she hadn't known existed.

"Are you okay?" he asked.

She blinked at the reserved demeanor of a man who two seconds ago had ripped at her clothes. He calmly buttoned his shirt and waited for her response. Except for the bulge in his black pants, he looked entirely unaffected by the episode. Just as he had when he'd kissed her at her parents' house.

The heavy meal lurched in her stomach and Alexa fought past the nausea. She took a deep yoga breath and sat up, pulling down her top. "Sure. Answer the door."

He stared at her for a few moments, as if checking to see if he believed her facade, then nodded and walked out of the room.

She mashed her fingers against her lips and tried to hold it together. She'd made a monumental mistake. Obviously, her recent celibacy had caused her hormones to go insane, until any man who touched her set her off like a firecracker. His last statement flashed in her mind with a mocking finality.

This means nothing.

She heard conversation in the hallway. A tall, leggy brunette entered the room with the ease of someone who knew the house well. Alexa stared at one of the most beautiful women she'd ever seen—obviously Nick's ex.

Chorus-girl legs started with black platform heels and disappeared under a pair of silk trousers. Her slim hips were encircled with a silver chain belt, and a metallic stretchy top molded to her small breasts, dipping at the neckline and exposing the top of her shoulders. Her long raven hair fell down her back in a mass of perfect waves. Not a frizzy curl in sight. Her eyes were a startling emerald color with long black lashes. Her full lips set off high cheekbones and she radiated an air of relaxed elegance. She looked around the room, then focused on Alexa.

Alexa knew then she was going to throw up.

The goddess turned to Nick with an air of apology. Even her voice was a husky reminder of sex. "I just had to meet her."

With horror, she realized Gabriella not only slept with Nick but actually cared about him. The obvious hurt shimmering in those eyes accused her woman to woman for stealing her man. Part of Alexa watched the scene from above with actual humor. It was like an episode of *The Real Housewives of New York City* gone horribly wrong. At least it wasn't *Jersey Shore*. Her crazy thoughts rocketed and she grabbed at the tendrils of her sanity.

Alexa rose and looked up at the skinny goddess who towered over her. She dug deep for composure and pretended she wore real clothes and not a gym outfit. "I understand," she said formally.

"Gabby, how did you get past security?"

Artfully tousled curls slid over one shoulder. Gabriella reached out and pressed something in Nick's hand. "I still had my key and the security code. After you told me you were going to marry, well, things got a bit intense."

The words pummeled Alexa's sensitive skin like wasp stings. To hell with this. She refused to allow Nick to continue a relationship on the side when they had signed a contract. Therefore, she needed to pretend to be the possessive wife. She swallowed hard and forced herself to smile calmly at her adversary.

"Gabriella, I'm sorry if you were hurt by our decision. It came rather fast for both of us, you know." She laughed and positioned herself between the two. "We knew each other from years ago and when we met again, we got caught up in a whirlwind." She pretended to look up with adoration at her current husband, though her fists ached to get one good punch in. He slipped his arms around her and his body heat burned through the thin material of her yoga pants. "I have to ask you to leave. It's our honeymoon night."

Gabriella studied them with an assessing air. "Odd you wouldn't be taking a trip somewhere more…romantic."

Nick saved her. "I have work obligations, so we delayed our island getaway."

Gabriella spoke in a clipped manner. "Fine. I'll leave. I needed to see for myself who he chose over me." Her expression informed Alexa she didn't understand Nick's decision. "I'll be out of town for a bit. I committed to help in Haiti with some of the rebuilding."

Oh. My. God. She was a humanitarian. The woman looked perfect, had money, and actually helped people. Alexa's heart sank. Gabriella turned and focused on the deck of cards. "Hmmm, I always loved cards. Just not for a wedding night."

Gabriella didn't give them a chance to reply. With the gracefulness of a cobra, she slithered out the door without a backward glance.

Alexa jumped away from Nick at the sound of the *click*. An awkward silence settled over the room as her thoughts spun.

"I'm sorry, Alexa. I never expected her to show up at my house."

The question rose from deep within. She swore she wouldn't ask, but the short and bloody battle had ended before it even began. The words sprang from her lips. "Why did you marry me and not her?"

Compared to Gabriella, Alexa lacked in every facet. Nick's girlfriend was beautiful, elegant, and skinny. She spoke with intelligence, volunteered for worthy causes, and actually behaved with class for a woman scorned. She also cared about Nick. Why would he have hurt her?

Nick stepped back. "It doesn't matter," he said coldly.

"I need to know."

Ice slithered down her spine as she caught the resolution on his face. The shutter slammed down, and suddenly she looked upon a man with absolutely no emotion or feeling. "Because she wanted more than I can give her. She wanted to settle down and raise a family."

Alexa took a step back. "What's so wrong about that?"

"I told Gabriella the truth from the beginning. I don't do permanent. I never want children, and I will never be the type of man to settle down long-term. I promised myself years ago." He paused. "So I married you instead."

The room spun as the finality of his statement washed over her. Her husband may experience fits of passion. His touch may be warm, and his lips even warmer, but his heart was carved in stone. He'd never let a woman inside—he was too badly damaged to take a chance. Somehow, his parents had convinced him love does not exist. Even if a weak ray glimmered on the surface, he still believed there was no happy ending. Just children as casualties and a lifetime of hurt.

How could any woman fight such a hardcore belief

with any hope of winning? His need for a business marriage suddenly made perfect sense.

"Are you okay?"

She decided to end the night with her finale. Nick Ryan could break her heart. Again. She needed to act cool and efficient in order to save her pride. And she must always keep her distance. Alexa schooled her features to give away nothing and pushed the pain deep inside her body until it was a tight ball in her stomach.

"Stop asking me if I'm okay. Of course I'm okay. Just don't think you can sneak in a quickie with your ex. A deal is a deal."

His face tightened. "I gave you my word, remember?"

"You also cheated at poker."

The reminder of their poker game gone awry made humiliation burn through her. He shifted his feet and pushed his hand through his hair and Alexa knew the speech was coming. "About what happened—"

She gave an Academy Award–worthy laugh. "Oh, Lord, we're not going to have a talk about *that*, are we?" She rolled her eyes. "Listen, Nick, I have to admit something. Sure, this marriage is a business arrangement, but I was wearing the dress, and it was technically our wedding night, and..." She threw her hands up in surrender. "I got carried away with the whole idea. You just happened to be, well—"

"Available?"

"I was thinking more...handy. You were handy. It didn't mean anything, so let's just blow the whole thing off, okay?"

He studied her with narrowed eyes, taking in every feature

of her face. The clock ticked and she waited. A strange play of emotion flickered in his eyes, until she swore he stared at her with regret.

It must have been a trick of the light.

He finally nodded. "We'll blame it on the wine and the full moon or something."

She turned. "I'm going to bed. It's late."

"Okay. Good night."

"Good night."

She walked up the spiral staircase and slid beneath the covers, not wanting to brush her teeth or do her skin routine or change into her pajamas. She pulled the downy comforter up to her chin, buried her face in the pillow, and embraced sleep, a place she didn't have to think or feel or hurt.

• • •

Nick looked at the deserted staircase. Emptiness pulsed inside him and he had no idea why. He poured the rest of the wine into his glass, adjusted the volume on the stereo, and settled onto the sofa. The opera music flowed over him and soothed his nerves.

His almost-mistake loomed before him. If Gabby hadn't shown up, Alexa would've been in his bed. No more uncomplicated marriage.

Stupid.

When had his need for a woman ever caused havoc with his plans? Even when he'd courted Gabriella and they'd become intimate, he'd never been attached to the outcome.

His goal was clear and necessary. But even that wasn't enough to stop him once he'd gotten a taste of Alexa McKenzie. She wrecked his mind, made him laugh, and tempted him with the delights of her body without a single subtle manipulation. She was different from any other woman he'd ever known, and he wanted her to stay in the category of his friend. His sister's best friend. He wanted to laugh at their past, live in harmony for one year, and say good-bye with ease.

The first lousy night he'd gone and ripped off her shirt.

He drained the glass of wine and switched the stereo off. He'd fix it. She already admitted she only wanted a warm body in her bed. Obviously, she wasn't attracted to him, and she'd probably drank too much wine and gotten caught up in the wedding fantasy. Just as she admitted. She wanted the money, and she missed the sex.

His stubborn mind screamed she couldn't react so passionately to every man who touched her. He firmly ignored the warning, moved from the couch, and headed up the stairs to his own bed.

Chapter Five

Alexa looked over the crowd and wished she were back at BookCrazy, holding her Friday night poetry reading. The business dinner tonight was the turning point in Nick's career. She knew heavy hitters swarmed the halls for the chance at glory, and Nick needed to dazzle the crowd in order to get a hearing.

She handed the hostess her coat and let Nick lead her into the packed ballroom. "I'm assuming you have a general plan of attack?" she asked. "Who are the two players you need to concentrate on?"

He motioned toward a thick cloud of cigar smoke. A tight circle of conservative businessmen surrounded a man impeccably dressed in a gray suit and silk tie. "Hyoshi Komo is building the Japanese restaurant. His vote is key to gain the third partner in the waterfront deal."

"So, why don't you go over there and give your pitch?" She plucked a salmon tart from the tray of a tuxedo-clad waiter and grabbed a glass of champagne from another.

"Because I don't want to be one of the crowd. I have a different plan in mind." She sipped the bubbly and sighed with pleasure. "Don't get drunk," Nick said.

She huffed out a breath. "I never knew husbands were so controlling. Okay, who's the final guy you need to impress?"

A flash of calculation crossed his face. "Count Michael Conte. He owns a successful pastry business in Italy and decided to try his luck in the States. He's focused on the first bakery opening at the waterfront."

She lusted after the tray of crab cakes on her left and tried to pay attention. Nick let out a huff, grabbed two from the waiter, and slid them on the plate. "Eat."

"Right." For once, she agreed with his order. She popped the cake into her mouth and groaned with delight. His brows snapped together and she realized she'd made him cranky. Again.

He stared at her mouth as if he wanted the crab cake for himself. "Alexa, are you listening?"

"Yes. Conte. Bakery. I guess you expect me to mingle while you do your business?"

He gave a tight smile. "I'll work on Hyoshi for now. Why don't you keep your eyes open for the count? He's tall, Italian accent, dark hair and eyes. Engage him in some conversation—it will keep you occupied."

A small nibble of warning teased the edges of her consciousness, but she was still too focused on the array of delicious appetizers. "You want me to talk to him?"

He shrugged in controlled carelessness. "Sure. Be nice. If you find out anything interesting, let me know."

A chill skated down her spine and suddenly the scene crystallized. "You want me to spy for you?"

Impatience flicked in his voice. "You're being ridiculous. Just relax and enjoy the party."

"Easy for you to say. Your boobs aren't hanging out of your dress."

Nick cleared his throat and shifted. "If you weren't comfortable, you shouldn't have worn the dress."

She stiffened. "I borrowed it from Maggie. I didn't have an expensive dress."

"I would have given you the money."

"I don't need your money."

"Somehow, I doubt that. You didn't sign the contract for any lofty reasons. Might as well take as much as you can get."

A short silence settled between them. Coldness seeped through her. "You're right. I was an idiot. Next time I'll buy out Macy's and send you the bill." She turned on her heel and tossed her head. "After all, the only benefit to this marriage is your money."

She walked away and left him staring at her back.

Jerk.

Alexa sipped a second glass of champagne and settled herself by the picture window overlooking the balcony. Nick Ryan belonged in this world—one of money and supermodels and refined dialogue. Clouds of Shalimar and Obsession blended with the heavy scent of cigar smoke. Her sight was blinded by an array of silks and satins, mostly in black or neutral—non-showy colors to set off the diamonds and pearls and sapphires she knew were all real. Everyone had sun-kissed skin, and she bet there wasn't a tan line in the lot.

Alexa heaved a deep sigh. She'd dressed with care for the party and held her breath as she walked down the stairs to await Nick's opinion. Even she knew she looked damn good in Maggie's dress. The thought that she actually wanted to please him pissed her off.

He'd given her a thorough once over. Instead of a compliment, he'd mumbled about her choice of wardrobe and walked away. Didn't even help her with her coat or spare her a second glance until they got to the party. Hurt sliced deep but she punished herself for the emotion. She retained a polite aura and pretended she dressed like this every Saturday night.

Yet, as soon as he spoke about his plan for the waterfront, his face shimmered with such raw emotion, her body clenched in response.

Passion. Fierce need burned in his golden brown eyes. She fantasized about being the woman who incited such wanting. Once again, she was reminded Nick only experienced strong emotions for his buildings. Never for women.

And never for her.

She took a deep breath and finished her drink. Then launched herself through the double doors of the balcony and approached a group of women who seemed to be commenting on the sculpture. Within moments, she neatly entwined her way into the discussion, secured introductions, and delved into the world of social chatter.

. . .

Nick watched her stalk across the room and cursed under his breath. Hell, he'd done it again. He should've complimented her on the damn dress. But nothing had prepared him for her entrance as she walked down the stairs, ready for the party.

The electric blue dress dipped low in the front, clung to the edge of her shoulders, and fell down to the floor in magnificent, flowing folds of shimmering material shot with silver thread. Strappy silver sandals encased her feet, her hot pink toenails peeking out and playing hide-and-seek as she walked. Her hair was pinned high on her head, with corkscrew curls tumbling around her ears and caressing the back of her neck. Her lips were painted red. When she blinked, her silver shadow threw sparkles over her lashes and caught the light. He bet she'd also catch the attention of every man in the place.

He'd almost ordered her to change. This was no cool sophisticate he could control. This was a full-blown Eve, who dared a man to Hell and made a poison apple seem as sweet as candy. Instead, he'd muttered some remark under his breath and let the subject matter drop. He wondered if that was a flash of hurt in her eyes, but when he looked again, she was the same troublesome, sarcastic woman he'd married.

Anger cut through him at her constant ability to make him feel like shit. He hadn't said anything wrong. She'd married for money and freely admitted it. Why did she have to pretend to play the innocent victim in this whole mess?

He forced thoughts of his wife out of his mind and concentrated on the group of businessmen circling Hyoshi

Komo. Nick sensed one important factor to secure the Japanese man's vote.

Excitement.

Get Hyoshi Komo excited, and Nick had the job.

The last and final piece in the puzzle was Michael Conte. The famous count was well known in the business world for his charm, money, and sharp intelligence. He believed in passion, not preciseness, and behaved completely differently from his other two partners. Nick hoped a lively conversation with his wife might help him gain a bit of an edge, especially since gossip pegged Conte as a womanizer. He stifled the quick flare of guilt and stepped into the group of men to speak.

. . .

Alexa decided it was time to find her husband.

Besides the brief time seated beside him at dinner, they'd been out of each other's company the whole night. Humming under her breath to the strains of "I Get a Kick Out of You," she checked the room but couldn't pick him out of the crowd. She decided to make her way down the elaborate hallway. Maybe he'd gone to the bathroom.

Her heels clicked against polished marble. The sounds of the music faded, and she studied the paintings on the wall with pleasure, murmuring to herself when she found one she recognized. Her steps carried her around the next corner into a room that looked more like a gallery, filled with shelves of old bound books carefully displayed. She held her breath as her fingers itched to caress the binding of old leather and relish the sound of crackling as she turned the pages steeped in history.

"Ah, so to get you to notice me tonight, I should turn into a book, no?"

She spun around. A man stood in the doorway, his eyes filled with a mischievous humor she knew to be a part of his core. His hair was long and caught back in a low ponytail, giving him the look of a pirate who had charmed women for centuries. His lips were full and his nose dominated his strong features in typical Italian style. Dressed in black pants, a black silk shirt, and expensive leather shoes, he exhibited a graceful, seductive air just by standing. Alexa knew immediately the man was charming, warm-hearted, and deadly to women. The thought made a smile curve her lips. She had a soft spot for womanizing Italian men. They reminded her of puffed-up peacocks who inwardly wished to be kept in line by the right woman.

"Oh, I noticed you." She turned her back and resumed her study of the books. "I knew you'd get to me by the end of the night."

"And were you looking forward to the moment, Signorina?"

"With baited breath. So, should we use one of the bedrooms here or go back to your place?"

A shocked silence descended.

Alexa peeked over her shoulder. A mixture of disappointment and temptation carved out his features. Alexa bet he missed the idea of a chase but didn't want to turn down such an offer. A delighted laugh bubbled to her lips at his obvious conflict and sudden loss of confidence.

A knowing light gleamed in his dark eyes. "You are teasing, no?"

She turned to face him, still laughing. "I guess I am."

He shook his head with amusement. "You are a wicked woman to tempt a man like that."

"You are a wicked man to think a woman would do such a thing."

"Perhaps you are right. A woman like you should have a husband watching at all times. Such a treasure could be stolen at any moment."

"Ah, but if I were a true treasure, I wouldn't be stolen easily. Certainly not by the first line thrown at me."

He pretended offense. "Signorina, I would never insult you by thinking it would not be a long treasure hunt. You'd require a lot of work."

"Signora," she corrected. "I am married."

His face pulled into a low, sad look. "Pity."

"Somehow, I think you knew."

"Perhaps. But let me introduce myself formally. I am Count Michael Conte."

"Alexa McKenz—er, Alexa Ryan."

He caught her slip-up and seemed to make a mental note. "Newly married, yes?"

"Yes."

"Yet you wander the hallways alone and were not seen in the company of your husband all night." He shook his head. "These American ways are tragic."

"My husband is here on business."

"Nicholas Ryan, correct?"

She nodded. "You should know him well. He's making a pitch for the waterfront deal."

Michael kept his face neutral. Obviously, behind his charming facade lurked a sharp businessman, and she bet he knew her identity when he approached. Nick underestimated Conte if he believed a conversation would soften him. This man obviously kept business and pleasure in two separate worlds.

"I have not had the pleasure of meeting him as of yet." He leaned in ever so slightly. His musky cologne rose in the air between them. His eyes met and held her own. She waited for a blast of sexual energy, a hum of chemistry, a note of hunger to shake her body and confirm Nick Ryan wasn't the cause of her problems.

Nothing. Not even a spark.

With a tiny inward sigh, she resigned herself to battling her attraction for Nick and admitted maybe she still harbored a crush from her girlhood days. If Michael Conte couldn't stir a shred of sexual emotion, she was in deep trouble.

Alexa sighed. "I think you will love my husband as much as I do," she said.

He received her message and accepted the implication with grace. "We shall see. As for us, we will be friends, no?"

She smiled. "Yes. Friends."

"I will accompany you back to the dining room for a cordial and you will tell me all about yourself."

She accepted his arm and allowed herself to be led out of the library. "You know, Michael, I think I have the perfect woman for you. She's a close friend of mine. And she may be your match."

"You underestimate yourself, signora." He gave a naughty wink. "I am still grieving your loss."

She laughed as they entered the dining room, then looked up in surprise when her husband stepped in front of them. He towered over her with an intimidating air. She opened her mouth to speak, but he reached out and pulled her into his embrace. A moment passed before she was able to form the words. "Hello, darling. I was chatting with Signore Conte. I don't think you two have formally met yet?"

The men sized each other up like they would just before a cockfight. Nick was the first to surrender. Probably for good business reasons and not anything to do with testosterone.

Nick offered his hand. "Michael, how are you? I see you've met my *wife*."

Michael shook his hand and Alexa studied her husband's expression with sheer puzzlement. Was she crazy, or did he not want her to engage Michael Conte with her sparkling conversation? Hadn't he hinted he wanted inside information if at all possible? Now he just looked plain irritated, as if she had betrayed him.

The clean scent of soap and lemon rose from his skin. His fingers splayed around her waist and rested on the curve of her tummy. She fought back a shudder when she imagined his hand coasting just a few inches downward. How would it feel to have his fingers deep inside her, taking her to places she ached to go but was too afraid to visit?

She refocused on their conversation.

"Congratulations, Nicholas. Alexa tells me you are

newlyweds. How difficult it must be to drag yourself to a business function, no?"

"Absolutely." His head lowered. Her breath hitched as his lips grazed her lobe, and his nose nuzzled her ear. Her nipples grew hard and tingly. She prayed her padded bra hid the evidence of her body's betrayal.

Michael watched the gesture with barely hidden amusement. "It seems Richard thinks you are the perfect man for the job. Perhaps we can set up a meeting to go over your ideas."

"Thank you. I'll call your secretary and arrange an appointment." She caught the clear-cut simplicity in his tone and knew Michael noticed. Nick didn't play certain business games, namely being too arrogant to pick up the phone himself to call for an appointment.

"Very good." Michael took her hand and placed a kiss on her palm. "It was lovely to meet you, Alexandria." His Italian accent caressed her name. "I'm having a dinner party for a few close friends two weeks from tonight. Would you join me?"

She noted he directed his invitation to her so she turned to her husband. "Darling? Are we free?"

This time, his movement wasn't subtle. He took a step behind her and wrapped both hands around her waist, drawing her back against him. Her butt pressed against his groin. Iron thighs trapped hers. He rested both hands directly under her breasts and spoke. "We'd love to come."

"Wonderful. I look forward to seeing you. Eight o'clock." He nodded to Nick and directed a smile toward her. "Have a good evening."

Within minutes of Michael leaving, Nick released her. The sudden loss of his body heat caused a chill to run down her spine. His face lost the look of a lover and turned impersonal. "Let's go."

Without another word, he strode toward the door, getting the coats from his hostess and saying his good-byes. She spoke to the few friends she had made and followed her husband to the car.

The lack of conversation continued during the drive home. Sick of the silent game, Alexa made the first move. "Did you have a good time?"

He grunted.

Alexa took that as a yes. "The food was really good, huh? And I was surprised at how nice some of the women were. I was invited to an art opening for Millie Dryer. Isn't that great?"

He snorted.

"How did business go? Were you successful tonight?"

He made another weird noise. "Not as successful as you, I guess."

Anger surged through her blood. Her voice strained with tension. "Excuse me?"

"Never mind."

Her fists clenched. The chill left her body and twisted into a fiery heat. "You're a hypocrite and a jerk. You asked me to seek Michael out and bring you back information. Do you think I'm stupid, Nick? You used me, but now you're pissed off. I did everything you wanted. Consider your favor completed."

"I only suggested you may be able to pick up something to help me with my business. I asked you to soften him up, not give him a hard-on that'll last for days."

He swung the car into the drive with a squeal of tires and cut the engine.

She sucked in her breath. "Screw you, Nick Ryan! He treated me with courtesy and never crossed the line once he found out I was married. But you're missing the big picture, Pretty Boy. Michael doesn't let business interfere with pleasure. I could've stripped off all my clothes and begged him to give you the contract and he wouldn't have budged. I can't help you with this one—you're on your own."

She got out of the car and stalked toward the house.

He cursed and trotted at her heels. "Fine. Then we don't have to go to his party. I'll just set up a business meeting."

She opened the door and tossed her head. "So, don't go. But I will."

"What?"

"I'm going. I liked him and I think his party will be fun."

Nick slammed the door, marched into the living room, and ripped off his tie. "You are my wife. You will not be going to any parties without me."

She wiggled out of her coat and hung it in the closet. "I'm a business partner who follows the rules. We're free to have our own lives as long as we don't sleep with anyone. Correct?"

He closed the distance between them and glared down at her. "I'm concerned about my reputation. I don't want him to get the wrong impression."

She lifted her chin and deliberately taunted him. "I'll

follow the rules of our deal but I'm going to Michael's party. It's been a long time since I've enjoyed a man's company. A man who is actually charming and funny and…warm."

Her last word exploded in the air between them. She watched in fascination as the calm man she knew turned into someone different. His clear eyes turned hazy, his jaw clenched, his body locked. His hands lifted until they grasped her upper arms. He looked like he was ready to shake her or do something else, something completely…irrational.

Her body lit up like an electrical current. Her lips parted to take in breath. And she waited.

"Do you need someone that badly, Alexa?" His mocking tone raked over her. He lowered his head so his mouth stopped inches from hers. With slow purpose, his hands moved from her arms and upward to circle her neck. Linking his fingers around the sensitive flesh, his thumbs tipped her head up, so he clearly spotted the wildly beating pulse her dress didn't hide. He watched her face while he continued the torture by tracing the line of her collarbone, the slope of her shoulders. Then moved lower. Both palms slid down her front and cupped her breasts in his hands. Excitement danced over her nerve endings. Her muscles softened and grew weak. Her breasts swelled and ached, rising to meet him. His thumbs grazed the tips, and a low groan rose from deep in her throat. He made a low murmur of satisfaction as he continued the stroking, teasing motions. She felt him harden, rise and press against the sensitive apex between her thighs. Liquid warmth rushed through her.

"Maybe I should give you what you need so badly." He

thrust his hips against hers to give her a taste, and she shook in response. His hands slipped under her dress, under her bra, and met warm, willing flesh. "Maybe if I took you now, you wouldn't need to go running to Conte." Her tummy plunged as those talented fingers plucked at her nipples and stroked her, his motions gentle and tender even as his words stung.

She trembled before him, a bundling mass of emotion and sensation, but her mind stayed icy clear. The truth of his actions forced her to play out her hand to win. Letting him win this battle would weaken her. He was going to kiss her. Right here, right now. He'd give her so much pleasure she'd beg for more, and he would leave her pride and sanity shredded. He wanted to kiss her for one reason—his power and manhood had been threatened, and he wanted them back. He didn't want *her*. The wild call of mating and male dominance beckoned him, and she was stuck in his path.

So, Alexa gathered up the scattered threads of her control and played her trump card.

She moved even closer and let her lips rest a bare inch from his. His breath rushed over her mouth.

"No, thank you," she whispered. She pulled his hands off of her. "I prefer we stick to business. Good night."

She turned her back on him and disappeared up the stairs.

• • •

Nick's hands hung at his sides, empty. For one moment, he'd been filled with her: her curves, her scent, her heat. Now he stood in the middle of the room, alone, just like he had on their wedding night. A married man with a hard-on and no relief in sight. Amazed at his ridiculous predicament, he tried to go over the events of the evening and see where he'd gone wrong.

The moment he caught her with Conte, a slow, steaming anger had risen up within him. The heat started at his feet, traveled to his stomach, his chest, and finally settled like a hot band around his head.

Her hand had rested on the count's arm. He must've been quite amusing, because she threw her head back and laughed, her cheeks flushed and rosy. Her full lips had gleamed under the chandelier light. They'd acted like they were longtime friends instead of people who had just met.

But the worst was when she smiled at him.

It was a dazzling, bewitching, come-hither smile that told the man on the receiving end he was everything she was looking for, everything she wanted. A smile that gave a man nasty dreams at night and haunted his waking hours. Nick had never seen that smile directed at him and something crazy exploded inside him.

His plan had misfired. He'd expected her to be mildly entertaining to the count and gain a few tidbits of knowledge to help close the deal. Not actually enjoy the man so openly.

Nick cursed and picked up his tie, ready to go to bed. As he climbed the stairs, he thought about what Alexa had said. If Conte did separate business and pleasure, he'd played the scene all wrong. Maybe when he requested a business meeting he'd concentrate on the rational logistics of the building rather than paint an emotional landscape for the sale. Maybe Conte was only passionate when it came to women. Maybe he wanted a cool-headed executive to head the architectural team.

Nick stopped at her door. The light was off. He paused for a moment and listened for her breathing. He wondered what she wore to bed. Images of scanty black lace wreaked havoc with his mind, but even the thought of her in flannel pants and a cropped T-shirt did things to him no other woman had ever accomplished. Was she lying awake in bed, dreaming of Conte? Or was she thinking about their last kiss and wanting more?

He walked to his own room. She'd rejected him. Her own damn husband. And he was stuck with the one thing he'd been horrified of.

A wife he was attracted to.

He shut his bedroom door and forced the thought out of his mind.

Chapter Six

Alexa sat at the table and faced her parents. Her hands shook with joy and relief as she pushed the check across the battered kitchen table that was covered in happy yellow plastic suns. "Nick and I want you to have this to pay off the mortgage," she announced. "There will be no arguments or protests. We talked about this for a long time, and we're lucky to have so much money. We want to share. It means a lot to us, so please accept this as our gift."

Their matching stunned expressions made tears prick her eyes. How many nights had she tossed and turned, feeling guilty for being unable to get her parents out of their financial mess? As the oldest sibling, she hated the helplessness that choked her. She decided dealing with Nick and her own burgeoning emotions was worth it. The payoff of security and safety for her family eased a deep ache, which she'd fought since her father had the heart attack.

"But how can you do this?" Maria pressed trembling hands to her lips as Jim put his arm around her. "Nick shouldn't feel like we're a burden. You're a young married couple with dreams. For your bookstore. For a family with lots of children. You shouldn't be taking care of us, Alexandria. We are the parents."

Jim nodded. "I already decided to take an extra job. We don't need the money."

She sighed at her parents' innate stubbornness. "Listen to me. Nick and I have plenty of money, and this is important to us. Dad, a second job isn't an option in your condition, unless you want to die. You heard the doctor." Alexa leaned forward. "This will give you the home free and clear so you can concentrate on paying the other bills. Save for Izzy's and Gen's college. Help Lance through his final year of medical school. We're not giving you enough to retire, guys, just enough to make things a bit easier."

They exchanged glances. Wild hope glimmered in her mom's eyes as she clutched the check. Alexa gave them a tiny nudge to push them over the edge. "Nick didn't want to come with me today. There's one condition to this money—he never wants to hear about it again."

Maria gasped. "I have to thank him. He needs to know how much we appreciate this—how he's changed our lives."

Alexa swallowed around the tightness in her throat. "Nick doesn't like to show a lot of emotion. When we discussed this, he insisted he never wants the money mentioned again."

Jim frowned. "He won't accept a simple thank-you? After all, if it weren't for me we wouldn't be in this mess."

"Anyone can get sick, Dad," she whispered.

The grief of the past ravaged his face. "But I left."

"And came back." Maria grasped his hand and smiled. "You came back to us and made it right. No more talk like this." Her mother straightened in her chair, eyes shining with emotion. "We will accept the check, Alexandria. And we'll never mention it to Nick. As long as you promise to go home and tell him he is our angel." Her voice broke. "I'm so proud you are my daughter."

Alexa hugged her. After a few more moments of conversation, she kissed both her parents and left the house. Poetry night was taking place at BookCrazy and she couldn't be late. She started her shuddering Volkswagen Bug and headed toward her store as her thoughts whirled.

The money ruse was unfortunate but necessary. She'd never admit to Nick how bad her parents' financial situation was. The image of him tossing a wad of money at her like enough bucks could solve any problem made her squirm. Her pride was important, and so was her parents'. They solved their own problems. She had an instinct that Nick Ryan believed money took the place of emotion, which was a lesson his parents had delivered on a daily basis. She shuddered at the thought.

No, she'd manage to do this on her own.

She settled down and drove to work.

. . .

Alexa glanced around BookCrazy with satisfaction. Poetry nights drew a large crowd, and all were book buyers. Every Friday night, she transformed the back of her store into a performance center. Moody background music floated through the dimly lit aisles. Overstuffed apple-green chairs and battered coffee tables were dragged from the storeroom and arranged in an informal circle. The crowd was a nice mix of intellectuals, some quite serious, and others who just wanted an entertaining night out. She dragged the mic over to the small lifted platform and checked her watch again. Five minutes to go. Where was Maggie?

She watched people settle into the chairs and mumble about coffee while discussing stanzas and imagery and the bleeding of emotion. On cue, the door opened to release a rush of brisk air, and Maggie stepped inside. "Java, anyone?"

Alexa raced over and grabbed two steaming cafe mochas. "Thank God. If I didn't serve them caffeine they'd read to one another in the Starbucks down the street."

Maggie set down the cardboard tray and lined up the cups. Her cinnamon-colored hair swung past her jawline when she shook her head. "Al, you're nuts. You know how much money you spend on coffee just so these artists can read poetry in front of one another? Let them get their own coffee."

"I need the business. Until I find a way to get a loan to expand the store, I need to keep them caffeinated."

"Ask Nick. He's technically your husband."

She shot her friend a warning look. "No, I don't want him involved. You promised you wouldn't say anything."

Maggie threw her hands up. "What's the big deal? Nick knows you'd pay off the loan."

"I want to do this on my own. I took the initial payoff and that was the deal. No more. It's not like this is a real marriage."

"Did you give the money to your parents?"

Alexa smiled. "Almost made the company of your brother worth it."

"I still don't get it. Why not just tell Nick the truth about the money? He's a pain in the ass but has a good heart. Why are you playing games, girlfriend?"

She turned away, afraid to confront her friend. She'd always been a sucky liar. How could she possibly tell Maggie she lusted after her brother and needed every barrier imaginable to keep her distance? If he believed she was a coldhearted money-grubber, he might leave her alone.

Maggie studied her face for a long time. Her green eyes filled with shock as the lightbulb suddenly flashed. "Is something else going on with you two? You're not attracted to him, are you?"

Alexa forced a laugh. "I hate your brother."

"You're lying. I always know when you lie. You want to sleep with him, don't you? Oh, yuck!"

Alexa snatched the last cup of coffee. "This conversation is over. I am not attracted to your brother, and he is not attracted to me."

Maggie followed close on her heels. "Okay, now that I'm over the initial grossness of the idea, let's talk about it. He's your husband, right? You might as well be getting sex for the next year with *someone*." Alexa walked to the platform. All eyes were now on her. *The word* sex *definitely gets people's attention*, she thought. She ignored her friend and made the initial introductions for poetry night.

As the first poet made his way onstage, she stepped aside and settled herself into her chair. She grabbed her notebook in case she needed to write down any nuggets of inspiration and cleared her mind for the reading.

Maggie knelt and whispered, "I think you should sleep with him."

Alexa let out a long-suffering sigh. "Leave me alone."

"I'm serious. I've now had a few minutes to think. It's perfect. You both have to be faithful anyway, so you know he won't be sleeping with someone else. This way you get the sex you need, and in a year, just say good-bye. No hard feelings. No complications."

She squirmed. Not because she was embarrassed by Maggie's suggestion. No, just the opposite. The possibility intrigued her. She lay awake at night, picturing him in the room down the hall. His naked, muscled body stretched out on the bed, waiting for her. Her hormones shook greedily at the image. Hell, at this rate she'd end up in a mental institution by the end of the year.

Cause: celibacy.

Maggie snapped her fingers in front of her face and jolted Alexa out of her reverie. "You disappeared on me again. Is Nick coming tonight?"

"Oh, yeah, your brother would just love this kind of night out. He'd probably prefer a root canal and a prostate exam."

"How are you two getting along? Besides the physical attraction."

"Fine."

Maggie rolled her eyes. "Lying again. You're not going to tell me, are you?"

Alexa realized she'd always confessed everything to Maggie except for one event. The first time Nick kissed her. She'd known she loved him back then. Friendship turned to rivalry and then to a girlish crush. That first kiss twisted emotions so pure within her she believed it was love. Her heart beat for him, full of joy at the possibility of them being together, so she uttered the words, her voice echoing through the trees.

"*I love you.*"

Then waited for him to kiss her again. Instead, he'd stepped back from her and laughed. Called her a silly baby and walked away.

She learned her first lesson in heartbreak in that moment. Fourteen years old. In the woods with Nicholas Ryan.

She wasn't about to repeat the lesson.

She pushed the memory away and decided to keep her second secret from Maggie. "There's nothing going on," Alexa repeated. "Can I listen to the next poem in peace, please?"

"I don't think peace is in the cards tonight, babe."

"What do you mean?"

"Nick's here. Your husband. The guy you're not attracted to."

She swung her head around and stared in shock at the figure in the doorway. He was obviously out of his element, but his presence was so confident, so overwhelmingly male, she sucked in her breath and realized the man had the power to fit in anywhere. And he wasn't even wearing black.

Most men who wore designer clothes allowed the fabric to dictate to them. Nick wore his Calvin Klein jeans as if he wore nothing at all. The denim hugged his thighs and hips as if folding to his will. He reflected a man who knew himself—and didn't give a damn what anyone else thought.

The turtleneck was a deep caramel cream in a thick cable knit stitch that emphasized his chest and stretched over broad shoulders. Definitely Ralph Lauren. The boots were Timberlands.

She waited as his gaze perused the room, skated over her, stopped, then came slowly back.

Their eyes met.

Alexa hated clichés, and what she hated most was becoming one. But at that moment, her heartbeat thundered, her palms sweated, and her belly dipped and plunged as if on a roller-coaster ride. Her body went on full alert, begging him to come to her, promising him surrender. If he told her to go home, get in bed, and wait for him, Alexa was sure she'd follow his instructions.

The weakness of her will infuriated her. Her honesty made her admit she'd do it anyway.

"Oh yeah. Definitely no attraction there." Maggie's words broke the weird spell and allowed Alexa to gather her composure. She had issued the invitation to Nick for poetry night because he hadn't seen her bookstore. He'd politely declined, citing work as an excuse, and she hadn't been surprised. Once again, she had reminded herself they came from different worlds, and Nick had no desire to visit hers. As he walked toward her, she wondered why he had changed his mind.

. . .

Nick picked his way through the bookshelves. Some guy dressed in black spouted into a microphone about the correlation between flowers and death, and the scent of cafe mochas rose to his nostrils. Sounds of a flute and the faint calling of a wolf drifted to his ears. All of his impressions were secondary to the sight of his wife.

Her true sexiness lay in her ignorance of her effect on men. Aggravation tickled his nerves. He lived in a constant state of emotional turmoil and he hated every moment. He was the calmest man around and dedicated his path to avoiding messy feelings. Now, his normal day ranged from annoyance to frustration to anger. She made him crazy with her wacko arguments and impassioned speeches. She also made him laugh. His home seemed more alive since she'd moved in.

He reached her. "Hi."

"Hi."

He directed his attention to his sister. "Maggie May, how goes it?"

"Fine, brother dearest. What brings you? You're not going to read that poem you wrote when you were eight, are you?"

Alexa tilted her head in interest. "What poem?"

He actually felt himself flush and realized the two women before him were the only ones who ever made him lose his composure. "Don't listen to her."

"I thought you had work," Alexa said.

He did. And he didn't know why he was there. He had left the office and entered an empty house and the silence bothered him. He'd thought of her surrounded by people in the bookstore she created and wanted to join her world for just a little while. He said nothing, though, and shrugged. "I wrapped up early. Thought I'd check out poetry night. Do all artists smoke? There's a long line outside and they're all puffing away."

Maggie snickered and stretched both of her legs out on the floor. Her back was propped up against the side of the chair. Her green eyes held the teasing light of a younger sister who still enjoyed torturing her older brother. "Still having cravings, Nick? Bet I could bum one for you."

"Thanks. It's always nice to have a family member as your drug pusher."

Alexa gasped. "You smoke?"

Nick shook his head. "Used to. Quit years ago."

"Yeah, but when he gets stressed or upset, he regresses. Do you believe he doesn't think it counts as long as he doesn't buy?"

Alexa chuckled. "This is very enlightening, guys. We need to get together more often. Tell me, Maggs, does your brother cheat at card games?"

"All the time."

Nick reached down and snagged Alexa's fingers, pulling

her up from the chair. "Show me the rest of the store while this guy finishes up."

Maggie chuckled and settled herself into the empty chair. "He's just afraid of what I'll tell you next."

"You're absolutely right."

Nick led her away from the crowd. With an instinctive motion, he stopped in a shadowed corner by a sign entitled RELATIONSHIPS. He guided her so her back pressed against the bookshelf, then dropped her hand. Nick shifted his feet and cursed under his breath at his sudden uneasiness. He hadn't planned what to say, just knew he had to break the tension between them before he got crazy and dragged her into his bed. Somehow, he needed to bring the relationship back to friendship. Back to older brother/younger sister camaraderie. Even if it killed him.

"I want to talk to you."

A slight smile twitched those bee-stung lips. "Okay."

"About us."

"Okay."

"I don't think we should go to bed with each other."

She threw back her head and laughed. Nick didn't know if he was annoyed at her amusement or fascinated by her open beauty. This was a woman who enjoyed life and gave out a full belly laugh. Not one of those calculated smiles or slight chuckles. Still, he hated when she laughed at him. Even though he was older, she dragged him back to a time when he was endlessly trying to be cool, and she thwarted every step.

"Funny, I don't remember offering you my body. Did I miss something?"

He frowned at her casual disregard of their problem. "You know what I'm trying to say. The night of the party got out of hand, and I take full responsibility."

"How chivalrous of you."

"Stop being a smart-mouth. I'm trying to tell you I was out of line and it won't happen again. I had too much to drink, I was pissed about Conte, and I took it out on you. I intend to stick to our original agreement, and I'm sorry I lost my control."

"Apology accepted. I'm sorry for contributing to the whole episode, too. Let's put it behind us."

Nick didn't like her terming such sexual heat as an episode, but he ignored the twinge. He wondered why he wasn't feeling relief at her easy agreement. He cleared his throat. "We have a long year ahead of us, Alexa. Why don't we try to build on friendship? It will be better for appearances and for us."

"What'd you have in mind? More poker games?"

An image of her sprawled in his lap flashed in his mind. Of full breasts pressed against his chest. Of squirming, soft female flesh all over him, ready to burn up in his arms. As if on cue, he looked up and read the title of the book right beside her in full presentation.

How to Give a Woman Multiple Orgasms.

Shit.

"Nick?"

He shook his head and tried to clear the fog. Was she multi-orgasmic? She shook in his embrace over a simple kiss. What would her body do if he gave her a full-blown sexual treatment, using his lips and tongue and teeth to push her over the edge? Would she scream? Would she fight her response? Or take it with pleasure and give it all right back?

"Nick?"

Sweat formed on his brow as he pulled his focus from the book and back to reality. He was a damn chump. Two seconds after stating they could be friends, he had her coming in his fantasies.

"Ummm, right. I mean, sure, we can play card games. Just not Monopoly."

"You always sucked at that game. Remember when Maggie made you cry when you landed on Boardwalk? You tried to bargain but she wanted cash. You didn't speak to her for a week."

He glowered. "You're thinking of Harold, the kid who lived down the street. I'd never cry at a game."

"Sure." Her crossed arms and expression told him she didn't believe him.

Aggravated, he dragged his fingers over his face and wondered how she made him lose it over a Monopoly game that never happened.

"So, we'll be friends. I can live with that," she said.

"Then it's a deal."

"Is that why you came to the poetry reading?"

He looked in her face and lied through his teeth. "I wanted to show you I can compromise."

He wasn't prepared for the sweet, sunny smile that curved her lips. She looked genuinely pleased, even though he admitted he'd done it for smooth sailing ahead.

She touched his arm. "Thank you, Nick."

Startled, he pulled back. Then fought embarrass-ment. "Forget it. Are you going to read tonight?"

Alexa nodded. "I better get back. I'm usually the last one. Go ahead and look around."

He watched her go back to the crowd and wandered through the shelves. He listened absently to the next poet, who recited lines through the muted wilderness music, and wrinkled his nose. God, he hated poetry. The spilling out of emotion, messy and unbridled, for any stranger to pick up and share. The convoluted comparisons between nature and rage, the endless clichés, and the confusing imagery made a man question his intelligence. No, give him a good biography or a classic like Hemingway. Give him the opera, where within the fierce emotions there was control.

A familiar, husky tone spilled over the micro-phone.

He paused in the shadows and watched Alexa take the small stage. She joked a bit with the crowd, thanked them for coming, and introduced her new poem.

"'A Small Dark Place,'" she said.

Nick prepared himself for high drama, and he'd already started forming some compliments in his mind. After all, it wasn't her fault he didn't like poetry. He was determined not to make fun of something so important to her, and he would even give encourage-ment.

"Hidden between soft fur and smooth suede;

My legs cramped and folded beneath me.

I wait for the end and for the beginning,

I wait for the bright, clean light to bring me back;

To the world of glittering colors and of perfumed scents that attack my nostrils;

To the world of sharp tongues, snaking out to shred soft smiles. I listen as ice tinkles against amber liquid.

Heat burns within, a reminder of a suicide from the past; a reminder of a silent murder.

Seconds...minutes...centuries...

The sudden knowledge twists my belly; I am home. I open my eyes to the blinding flash of a door opening.

And wonder if I will remember."

Alexa folded the piece of paper and nodded at her audience. Silence settled over everyone. Some people wrote feverishly in their notebooks. Maggie gave a whoop. Alexa laughed and stepped off the stage, and then she began to gather empty cups and chat as the night came to a close.

Nick stood alone and watched her.

A strange emotion bubbled up inside of him. Since he'd never experienced it before, he couldn't seek out a name. There was little left in life that touched him, and he admitted he liked it that way.

Tonight, something changed.

Alexa had shared an important part of herself with a room of strangers. With Maggie. With him. Open for criticism, vulnerable to the whims of others, she took what she felt and made him feel it, too. Her courage stole his breath. And as much as he admired her, doubt rose up inside of him like a monster out of a swamp and he wondered if beyond all his rationalizations, he was just a coward.

"What'd you think?"

He blinked at Maggie, then tried to focus. "Oh. I liked it. I've never heard her work before."

Maggie grinned like a proud Cub Scout mother. "I keep telling her she can get an anthology published, but she doesn't seem interested. Her real passion is BookCrazy."

"Can't she do both?"

Maggie snorted. "Sure. You and I would do it in a heartbeat, because we never miss an opportunity. Al is different. She's happy just by sharing—she doesn't need the glory of publication. She's been printed in some magazines, and she goes to a critique group, but that's more for the others than for her. That's our problem, bro. Always has been."

"What?"

"We're better at taking. Part of our childhood screwups, I guess." They both watched Alexa as she escorted her patrons out the door with her usual good humor. "But Al found her way by doing the opposite. There's nothing she won't do for someone."

Maggie suddenly turned on him. Her eyes blazed with a fierceness he remembered from the old days. Her finger jabbed into his chest. "One warning, pal. I love you dearly, but if you hurt her, I'll personally kick your ass. Got it?"

Instead of rising to the bait, he surprised himself by laughing. Then he dropped a quick kiss on her forehead. "You're a good friend, Maggie May. I wouldn't be so quick to judge yourself as a taker. I just hope the right guy sees that one day."

She stepped back. Her mouth dropped open. "Are you drunk? Or an imposter? Where did my big brother go?"

"Don't push your luck." Nick paused and glanced around the bookstore. "What's going on with the expansion?" He watched his sister's eyes widen, and he held back a chuckle. "Don't worry—it's no longer a secret. Alexa admitted she wants the money to add a café. I gave her the check but figured she'd ask me for a consult." His sister blinked and refused to speak. Nick frowned. "Cat got your tongue, Maggie May?"

"Oh, shit."

He quirked a brow. "What's the matter?"

Suddenly, she busied herself with the lone coffee cups and cleaning up the table. "Nothing. Umm, I think she may be embarrassed because she's hiring someone else to do it. Didn't want to bother you."

He fought a surge of annoyance. "I have time to help her."

Maggie laughed but it had an odd, desperate tone. "I'd leave it alone, bro. Gotta go. See ya."

She took off in a flurry. Nick shook his head. Maybe Alexa didn't want him involved in her project. After all, she had cited many times the fact that their relationship was based on a business contract.

Just as he had wanted.

He made a note to bring it up later. He helped lock up and walked his wife to her car. "Did you have dinner?" he asked.

She shook her head. "No time. Want to pick up a pizza on the way?"

"I'll throw something together for us at home." His tongue tripped on the last word. Oddly, he'd started to think of his sanctuary now as partly hers. "Won't take long."

"Okay. See you at home." She turned, then spun around. Opened her mouth. "Oh, Nick, don't forget—"

"The salad."

Her eyes widened, and her powers of speech seemed to desert her for a moment. She pulled herself together with a speed he admired. And she didn't even question how he knew. "Right. The salad."

Then she turned and walked to her car. Nick began to whistle as he made his way toward his BMW. He was definitely learning. He liked catching her by surprise. About time he got the upper hand.

He whistled most of the way home.

Chapter Seven

Nick shut the door behind him and fell into the leather chair. He stared at his drawing board and curled his hands into tight fists to stop the itch. He wanted to create. He envisioned materials such as limestone and brick, with flowing images of glass and sleek curves. The pictures danced behind his closed lids at night, and here he was, owner of Dreamscape Enterprises, and stuck most of the day in board meetings.

He cursed under his breath. Okay, so the board members aggravated him, with the pencil-pushing tactics and money-grubbing ideas. Most of them opposed the waterfront contract, believing the company would go bankrupt if he took the job and couldn't deliver. The board was right. He had a simple solution.

Don't fail.

Conte's party was Saturday night and he still hadn't secured a business meeting. Hyoshi Komo hadn't called, either. Stuck at square one, he knew the only thing to do was wait for the man to make his move and count down the hours to the party. Maybe Conte wanted to see how the social function turned out before seeking a meeting, unlike what he had told Alexa.

Alexa.

Her name alone was a punch in the gut. He remembered the way she had shrieked and shook her head and bounced around the living room in a victory dance after winning chess the night before. A grown woman acting like a child. And once again, he had laughed his ass off. Somehow, as beautiful as his companions were, their slick wit only rippled the surface. Alexandria made him connect with a deep belly laugh, like he was young.

His direct line buzzed. He picked up. "Yes?"

"Did you feed the fish?"

Nick closed his eyes. "Alexa, I'm working."

She made a rude snort. "So am I. But at least I worry about poor Otto. Did you feed him?"

"Otto?"

"You kept calling him Fish. That hurt his feelings."

"Fish don't have feelings. And yes, I fed him."

"Fish certainly do have feelings. And while we're discussing Otto, I wanted to tell you I'm worried about him. He's placed in the study and no one ever goes in there. Why don't we move him into the living room where he can see us more often?"

Nick dragged a hand down his face and prayed for patience. "Because I don't want a fish tank ruining the look of the main rooms. Maggie gave me the damn thing as a joke and I hated it on sight."

Frost nipped through the receiver. "Messy, too, aren't they? I guess you don't do humans or animals. I'm sorry to inform you, but even fish get lonely. Why don't we get him some company?"

He straightened and decided to put an end to this ridiculous conversation. "No. I don't want another fish, and he will not be moved. Do I make myself clear?"

The line hummed. "Crystal."

Then she hung up.

Nick cursed, grabbed the nearest stack of papers from the last board meeting, and got to work. The woman actually bothered him at his job about a fish.

He pushed the image of her out of his mind and resumed his work.

• • •

"He's gonna be mad."

Alexa bit down on her lower lip and wondered why Maggie's words caused a chill to run down her spine. After all, Nick Ryan was no alpha male. Sure, he'd be a little put out from the situation, but he always remained rational.

She surveyed the living room filled with dogs. Lots of dogs. Puppies and mutts and purebreds and hound dogs. Some crowded the kitchen, bumping into tables as they ate their food and slurped water. Others kept up a furious pace as they explored their new home, sniffing in corners and moving from room to room. The wire-haired terrier chewed on a throw pillow. The black poodle jumped on the couch and settled down for a nap. The mutt looked about ready to lift his leg by the speaker, but Maggie grabbed him and threw him into the backyard before he did serious damage.

The worry blossomed into a full-fledged panic attack.

Maggie was right.

Nick might kill her.

She turned toward her friend. "What should I do?"

Maggie shrugged. "Tell him the truth. You're only taking them for a night or two until the shelter can make other arrangements. If you give them back, they'll all be put to sleep."

She winced. "What if he still makes me get rid of them?"

"Take them to your apartment."

"Too small."

Maggie threw up her hands when she spotted the look. "Hell, no, I'm not taking them to my place! I've got someone coming over and he'll be a lot warmer than a puppy. You're on your own."

"But Maggs—"

Maggie gave a wave. "Gotta go. Man, I'd love to see the show when my brother walks in. Call me on my cell."

The door shut.

Alexa surveyed the room, now in puppy chaos, and decided she'd been a little too impulsive. She could have reasonably told the shelter she'd take a few, then brought them to her apartment. But no, she'd been mad at Nick for being a coldhearted monster about the fish and decided to teach him a lesson. Except now she was just plain scared.

The hound dog gnawed at the table leg. She pulled herself together and prepared her battle plan. She'd put them all in the spare room and maybe Nick wouldn't notice. He never went in that room. She'd bring all their toys and food and sneak them out the back for their walks. She convinced herself the strategy would work and herded the group down the hall. She dumped out a whole bag of play toys and made sure most of the dogs ran after them. Then she shut the door and gathered up the sleeping puppies on the couch, the food and water bowls, and some spare newspapers. She raced out and got the last stray from the backyard and set up the room so the dogs would be comfortable.

Alexa stared worriedly at the beautiful love seat and chair in swirling patterns of silver and gray. Damn, why did Nick have to be rich? No one's spare room looked this good, with slate carpeting, pewter tables with ornate scrolling, and throws that cost more than her whole comforter set at home. She ran her fingers over the soft, precise stitches of an afghan. She needed some old blankets, and she bet her husband didn't have one. She decided to go on a hunt upstairs when she heard the key in the lock.

Panicked, she threw the afghan over the chair and shut the door behind her. Then she hurled herself down the hallway and skidded to a stop in front of him. "Hi."

He looked suspicious already. Blond locks slipped over his forehead and his eyes narrowed, as if he didn't trust her to be nice. Guilt squirmed within, but she ignored the emotion.

"Hi." He looked around the house and she held her breath. "What's going on?"

"Nothing. I was just about to cook dinner. Unless you're tired and want to go to bed right now."

One brow shot up at her hopeful tone. "It's six o'clock."

"Right. Well, I bet you have a lot of work to do, huh? I'll bring your food upstairs to your office if you want."

Now he looked plain irritated. "I did enough work today. I want to relax with a glass of wine and watch the ball game."

"Are the Mets on?"

"Don't know. They're not in the playoffs anyway and they didn't make the wild-card. The Yanks still have a chance."

She squirmed with pent-up annoyance. "They're too far back—it'll never happen. New York won't be getting in the series this year."

He let out an impatient breath. "Why don't you watch the Mets upstairs?"

"I want the big TV."

"So do I."

Crankiness hit her hard. Alexa grabbed onto the emotion, grateful the fear had melted away. She turned her back and stalked into the kitchen. "Fine, I'm calling in my favor."

He hung his black wool coat in the closet, then stood in the doorway. She took out ingredients for the salad she wouldn't eat and cut up vegetables for a stir-fry. He grabbed a bottle of wine from the refrigerator and poured her a glass. "What did you say?"

"I'm calling in my favor. I want to watch the Mets game downstairs on the big TV. I want you to stay upstairs and watch the Yankees game, and I don't want to hear a sound. Not a cheer, or a yell, or a 'Go Yankees' rally. Got it?"

When she looked back, he gaped at her in sheer amazement, as if she'd sprouted horns. She tried to ignore how adorable he looked, with his mouth slightly open and those incredible shoulders stretched against the pale gray down shirt. Why did he have to be so damn attractive? The shirtsleeves and collar were still crisp after hours of wear. His charcoal pants still held the crease down the middle. He had unfastened the buttons by the wrists and rolled the material up in his usual fashion. Light-colored hair sprinkled over his forearms and strong fingers gripped the delicate wine glass with a power that made her fidget when she thought of the other things he could touch. She tried not to ogle him like a teenager and focused on chopping.

"You're insane." He actually took a few moments to gather his powers of speech before continuing. "These favors are supposed to be used for important things."

"My choice. My favor."

He stepped closer. His body heat pulled and tantalized and tortured her mental sanity. She ached to lean back against his chest and let his arms clasp around her waist. She craved to feel all that muscled strength support her and pretend they were a real-life married couple. They'd neck in the kitchen and make love on the heavy oak table amidst the wine and pasta. Then share dinner and talk quietly and watch the Mets game together. Alexa forcibly swallowed the lump in her throat and pushed away the fantasy.

"You're using a favor in order to watch a lousy baseball game?"

"Yep."

She threw the garlic and peppers in the skillet and he moved another inch. His belt rasped against her buttocks. Even though she was covered in thick denim, the threat of a more intimate touch made her hands tremble around the knife. His breath rushed warm against the nape of her neck. He placed both palms flat on the countertop and caged her in. "Favors are rare. Want to waste it on a stupid ball game that doesn't mean anything?"

"I care about every game the Mets play. You, on the other hand, don't take it as seriously because you're complacent. Winning comes too easily. You take it for granted."

He growled in her ear. "I don't win all the time."

She stuck to the topic of baseball. "Even after losing the ALCS championship game to the Sox, you never lost your arrogance. Still didn't respect another team."

"Never knew the poor Yanks caused such a fuss."

"It's the fans more than the team. We Mets fans know what it's like to lose. And each game we win is a small victory we appreciate and never take for granted. We're also more loyal."

"Hmmm. Talking Mets or their fans?"

"See, you think it's funny. If you experienced loss more, you'd be humbled. The win would feel even sweeter."

He rested his hands on the curve of her hips. The length of his erection pressed against her rear. "Maybe you're right," he murmured.

The knife clattered on the chopping block. She spun around and bumped against his chest. He caught her by the shoulders and tipped her chin up. Sensual tension swirled and crested. Her lips parted in unconscious invitation at his admission. "What?"

A savage glint appeared in the depths of his tawny eyes. "Maybe I'm starting to appreciate things I can't have." He ran one finger roughly down her cheek. Traced her lower lip. Pressed his thumb over the sensitive center of flesh. "Maybe I'm starting to learn about wanting."

Her mouth went dry. She ran her tongue over her lips to dampen them, and the sensual tension twisted another notch. She poised on the edge of some discovery that would change their relationship, and she battled her instinct to jump over the cliff, to hell with the consequences.

Instead, she forced herself to continue their odd conversation. "So, you agree? You understand why the Mets are a better team?"

A flash of straight white teeth mocked her statement. "No. The Yankees are a better team. They win for one reason." He whispered his comment against her lips. "They want it more. If you want something badly enough, Alexa, you eventually take it."

She shoved at his chest and spun back around, wanting to brandish the knife on more than the vegetables. Typical arrogant Yankee fan. "I'll call when dinner's ready. Until then, I expect you'll be upstairs."

His laughter echoed through the kitchen. The chill settled around her as he walked away. Alexa held her breath as he started up the stairs, but the dogs were still quiet.

She raced into the living room, put on the baseball game, pumped up the volume, and went into the back room to check on the canines.

The afghan was torn to shreds.

She pried it out of the black lab's teeth and stuck it in the bottom desk drawer. The paper was already dirty, so she cleaned up, spread fresh newsprint down, and laid some over the couch and chair for extra insurance. She refilled the water bowls and figured they'd all have to go out again in another hour before bedtime.

She shut the door, sped into the kitchen, and finished dinner while shouting loud comments to her players.

Nick came down for his dinner and quickly went back upstairs. Exhausted from her trickery, she vowed from now on to be honest with the shelter.

She managed to sneak the dogs out in small groups for the rest of the evening.

When the game ended and the Mets had won 4-3 over the Marlins, she did a quick victory dance, cleaned the kitchen, checked on the animals, and climbed the stairs to bed. Her muscles ached and her head spun, but she had been victorious.

She'd need to wake up before five a.m. to get all the animals walked, fed, and cleaned up before Nick left for work.

She winced but managed to shower quickly and fall into bed. She didn't even bother with a nightgown but crawled immediately under the comforter and fell asleep.

. . .

Someone was in the house.

Nick sat up in bed and listened. A faint scraping noise

echoed through the air. As if someone scratched a key against a lock and tried to jimmy the door open.

With quick, economical motions, he padded on bare feet to the door and opened it an inch. Silence greeted him. Then he heard the sound.

A low murmur. Almost like a growl.

A chill ran down his spine and he thought over his options. Who the hell was in his house? The alarm hadn't gone off, which meant the burglar had disarmed it. He didn't have a gun or a bottle of mace. What else was used in the Clue game? A revolver, candlestick, knife, rope, or lead pipe.

Better off calling 9-1-1.

He eased out of the doorway and tiptoed past Alexa's closed door. He paused, then decided waking her would be the wrong thing to do—she may panic or give the intruder a target Nick didn't want to deal with. His main goal right now was to keep her safe. He grabbed a baseball bat from the hall closet, swept up the cordless phone, punched out the three numbers, and reported a break-in.

Then he started down the stairs to hurt the son of a bitch.

Nick stopped at the bottom and hid in the shadows. The air remained still except for the steady buzz of the refrigerator. He stood alone for a while and studied the darkened rooms. The front door was solidly locked—chain hooked on, alarm set. Strange. If it had been disarmed, the red light would be out. Maybe the back door, but he hadn't heard the panes of glass break, unless—

The door to the spare room rattled. He eased forward, keeping tight against the wall, baseball bat brandished while he counted down the seconds before the cops would arrive. Clint Eastwood he was not, but if he got one good hit with the bat, he could call himself a man.

Heavy breathing. Almost like a pant. A scratch.

What the hell?

He stopped and reached for the knob. His pulse skittered with a rush of adrenaline. He fought past the fear and latched onto control. Nick raised the bat, turned the knob, and threw open the door with all his strength.

"Aaaaghhh!"

A group of dogs rushed past him. Two, four, six, eight—a crowd of fur encircled his legs. Spotted dogs, little dogs, big dogs—all barking and wagging tails and lolling tongues. The bat hovered high in the air but they never sensed danger. Thrilled to see a human in the dark hours of the night, they all leaped to attention and wanted to play.

For a few seconds, he convinced himself he was having a dream and would wake up in his own bed.

Then he realized the scene was real.

And a murder would be committed.

Involving his wife.

The room was in shambles. Shredded papers flew in every direction. The luxurious carpet was mottled with liquid circles that didn't look like water. Stuffing poked out of a couch cushion. His potted plant laid drunkenly to one side and one puppy pawed through the pile of dirt. *Architectural Digest* had been chewed up and spit out.

Nick closed his eyes. Counted to three. Opened them.

Then screamed his wife's name at the top of his lungs.

Right on cue, she launched down the stairs in a panic. When she saw the problem in front of her, she tried to back off, but she was running too quickly. Her bare feet skidded on the floor and she hit his body full force. With a whoosh of air released from her lungs, she grabbed onto his shoulders for balance and looked into his face.

She must have realized the danger within seconds. Those baby blues widened in pure fear and she stumbled back with her arms outstretched as if to ward off an attacker. Nick barely registered the movement. He was too intent on squinting through the haze of red that blurred his eyes.

One furry paw landed smack on his groin. He pushed it away and managed a furious whisper. "What the hell is going on?"

She winced. "Nick, I'm sorry. I didn't know what to do because the shelter called and said they were full and asked if I'd take a few for the night, and I couldn't say no, Nick, I couldn't or they would be put to sleep because the funding is so hard for the shelters nowadays, but I know you hate animals so I just thought they'd spend a quiet night here and go home in the morning."

"You thought you could hide a room full of dogs from me?" He tried desperately to control the rage this time, he really did, but he felt his voice getting higher. Then he understood why cavemen dragged women around by their hair.

He watched her face gauge his reaction. Her teeth reached for her bottom lip, and she did a little hop from leg to leg as if thinking really hard of how to explain things in a way that wouldn't make him madder.

A stray bone landed on his bare foot. He looked down at a lolling tongue and wagging tail.

"He wants you to throw it."

Nick glared. "I know what the damn dog wants; I'm not an idiot. Contrary to what you must think of me, that is. You used your favor to keep me locked upstairs so I wouldn't find out about this." He took in her guilty expression. "You're a good liar, Alexa. I guess I never knew how good."

She stopped cowering and pulled herself to full height in her bare feet. "I had to lie! I'm living with an animal hater who'd rather see innocent puppies in the gas chamber than mess up his house!"

Nick gritted his teeth and swore. "Don't try to turn this around on me, woman. You never even asked, just snuck a bunch of dogs into my spare room. Did you see what they did to my house? And where's my orange afghan?"

She threw back her head and made a frustrated wail. "I should have known you care more about your stupid possessions than a life! You're just like the guy from *Chitty Chitty Bang Bang*—remember he used to lock away all the children so the city would be neat and clean and organized? Heaven forbid everything didn't go exactly the way he wanted it. Let's keep life tidy. Let's make sure the orange afghan doesn't get ruined."

His temper teetered on the edge.

Then snapped.

His fists clenched and he let out a roar, which the dogs must have liked because they all started to howl at the same time and bounced around his feet in a whirl of fuzz and tails and paws.

"*Chitty Chitty Bang Bang*? You're insane—you need to be locked up in the loony bin. Lie to me, wreck my house, then compare me to a children's villain, all because you can't be a normal person and take responsibility and apologize?"

She stood on tiptoes and got right in his face. "I tried but you're being unreasonable."

He reached out and gripped her upper arms. His fingers closed around something silky and he shook her slightly. "Unreasonable? *Unreasonable*? It's the middle of the night and I'm standing in a room full of dogs, talking about a stupid movie!"

"It's not stupid. Why couldn't you be more like Ralph Kramden from *The Honeymooners*? Sure, he was loud and obnoxious, but he saved the whole shelter of dogs when he found out they would be destroyed. Why can't you be more human?"

"*The* friggin *Honeymooners* now? That's it, I've had enough. You are going to pack up every one of those dogs and take them back to the shelter right now, or God help me, Alexa, I'll get rid of them myself!"

"I won't do it."

"You will."

"Make me."

"Make you? *Make* you?" His fingers twisted around a wad of silky, satiny fabric as he fought for a shred of control. When the haze finally cleared his vision, Nick blinked and looked down.

Then realized his wife was naked. Her lime-green robe had slid down over her shoulders and now gaped open. Her sash had slipped unnoticed to the floor. He expected to catch a glimpse of some lacy negligee made to incite a man's lust. He got much more.

Jesus, she was perfect.

No fabric marred the endless curves of warm, gilded flesh. Her breasts were lush and made for a man's hands, her nipples the color of a ripe strawberry that begged for a man's tongue. Her hips formed the ancient hourglass figure artists based fantasies on instead of sharp bones that dictated the current fashion. Miles of long legs. A tiny scrap of fire-engine-red panties was the only thing that blocked his view.

The words died in his throat. His breath stopped, then rushed out like he'd been punched in the gut. She screwed up her face to keep yelling but paused when she noticed the change in his expression. Nick knew the moment she realized her robe had dropped. Knew when the knowledge she was naked hit her full force. Watched her lips purse a small circle of horror right before sanity hit to make her reach for the robe.

Nick used his two-second time span to make a decision.

Her fingers started to yank up the material when he blocked her motion, lowered his head, and stamped his mouth over hers. Shock held her immobile and he used this to his advantage. One quick thrust parted her plump lips and allowed him entry—entry to every slick, feminine, heated corner of her mouth. Drugged on the taste of her, he circled her tongue with quick, urgent strokes, begging her to give it all back to him.

And she did.

Full power.

As if a tightly closed door opened under a sharp kick, Nick almost heard the shatter as their control broke. She opened her mouth and drank, then made her own demands as a low growl of hunger escaped her lips. He pushed her hard against the wall and challenged each thrust of her tongue as her arms wrapped around his neck and her back arched. Her breasts tilted upward for full offering. His head spun as her flavor swamped his senses. His hands came around to cup her heavy breasts, and his thumbs rubbed her tight nipples. He became mad for the feel and taste and sight of her. A mass of dogs swarmed around their ankles, their crazed barking just a secondary noise to the roar in his blood.

He tore his mouth from hers to sink his teeth into the delicate line of her neck. A shudder wracked her body, and he made a low murmur of satisfaction as he moved lower to feast on her breasts, his tongue delicately licking the tip, nibbling, while she squirmed against the wall and urged him on. His mouth opened over her and he fed, sucking hard on her strawberry nipple as his hands slid around her back to grasp the curve of her buttocks, forcing her hips up to cradle the length of throbbing, hard flesh begging for entry.

"Nick, I—"

"Don't tell me to stop."

He looked up. Her breasts were slick from his mouth, her nipples tight and aroused by his attentions. Her belly quivered. Swollen lips parted, allowing panted, ragged breaths to escape. Her eyes darkened to a deep, drowning blue as her gaze locked on his. A second passed as he waited. A moment. A century.

"Don't stop."

She pulled his head down and kissed him. He ravaged the flesh of her lips as if he were imprisoned and she was his last taste of freedom, felt himself sink into the depths of her body until...

"Police!"

The sound of sirens fought its way into the sensual world they created. The door banged with command—the flashing red alarms spun a whirl of color through the windows and into the hall. The barking of the dogs grew louder with the commotion.

He staggered back from her as if coming out of a long stupor. She blinked, then with almost mechanical movements reached for her robe. Nick turned and headed toward the door, disarmed the alarm, and let his hand pause on the knob.

"You okay?"

She shuddered but managed to speak. "Yes."

He opened the door to a uniformed cop. Nick's drugged eyes and obvious arousal must have seemed suspicious, because the cop peeked down the hall to the robed woman and crowd of dogs about her feet. He holstered the weapon. "Sir, you reported a break-in."

Nick wondered if this moment was about to challenge his most embarrassing. He pushed a hand through his mussed hair and grabbed for his usual, logical sequence of thought. "Right. I'm sorry, officer, there's been a mistake. Please come in."

He knew if he didn't let him in it would look bad. The cop took the scene in with a glance and seemed to note the woman appeared willing and the dogs weren't trying to protect her from a maniac. He tipped his head. "Ma'am."

She swallowed hard. "Officer. Sorry about this." As if she knew Nick was also a bit foggy, she attempted the explanation. "My husband thought someone was in the house but it's all my fault. I hid these dogs in the spare room, hoping he wouldn't find out, and they must have made some noise in the middle of the night and he thought it was an intruder."

Nick closed his eyes.

Definitely an embarrassing moment.

He tried to interrupt. "Alexa, why don't we just—"

"No, Nick, let me finish. You see, officer, my husband doesn't like animals and I volunteer for the shelter so sometimes I take strays in and this time I didn't want him to find out about it so I tried to sneak the dogs into a place he wouldn't notice."

The cop turned his head politely. "You didn't notice a room full of dogs, sir?"

Nick ground his teeth in irritation. "She made me stay upstairs."

"I see."

"So, anyway, my husband heard the dogs and called 9-1-1 but when he tried to check the scene out himself he found the dogs and got mad and started yelling and I came down and we had a bit of a fight and then you showed up."

The cop glanced at the bat on the floor. "Sir, you were trying to surprise a burglar with nothing but a baseball bat?"

Nick wondered why he suddenly felt like the one accused.

He shrugged. "I called the cops but I figured I'd try to get the thug myself."

"You don't own a gun?"

"No."

"I'd recommend next time you think there's an intruder, call 9-1-1, lock yourself and your wife in a room, and wait for the police."

Steam rose but he forced a nod. "Of course."

The cop made some notes on his pad. "Ma'am, will you be okay tonight with the dogs?"

"Yes, we'll be fine."

"Then I'll be on my way. Let me take some information for my report." He took down the basics, then paused to pat the black lab on the head. A smile touched his lips. "Cute dogs. You're doing a wonderful thing, Mrs. Ryan. I'd hate to see any of these animals put to sleep."

She practically beamed up at him in her lime-green robe and ravaged, tangled hair. "Thank you."

"Good night." With a polite nod, he let himself out.

Nick shut the door behind him, then turned to face his wife.

• • •

Alexa wasn't about to wait for his tidy explanations. She bet a long list of excuses hovered on the tip of his tongue. He'd been mad and lost control. Sleep deprivation caused him to reach for her and damn the consequences. Now that the police had doused him with a jolt of cold water, he'd gone over the idea and decided it would not be in their best interests to sleep with each other. After all, it was in the contract. After all, this was a business marriage.

After all, this wasn't real.

The sexual fog drifted away and left her with a dull, nagging pain. She looked upon the policeman as Fate—her Earth Mother finally stepping in to lend a helping hand.

"Alexa—"

"No." She put up one hand and Nick went quiet, waiting. Alexa knew, right then and there, she had very dangerous emotions for Nicholas Ryan. Messy, real-life feelings. She took the truth like a dose of bitter medicine and met the fact head-on. If she slept with him, things would turn for her and would remain the same for him. She'd fall in love, and he'd have a good time. She'd be broken-hearted at the end of a year, and he'd walk away without a glance back. Another piece of information hit her like a knockout to the head.

If he asked, she'd go to bed with him.

She practically shuddered with shame. She had no control over her hormones when he touched her. She couldn't even promise she'd never consider the opportunity in the future. But she knew one thing—the only way she'd go to bed with her husband was if he begged. She wanted him mad for her, hot and explosive and so horny just a touch would push him over the edge. Like tonight. But she wanted no more excuses of temper, or sleeplessness, or alcohol. She wanted straight-out, fabulous, passionate sex with his head clear and his eyes on her. Not thinking about Gabriella. And not thinking about an end to celibacy.

She needed him to want only her.

That was the last proverbial nail in her coffin. Because tonight, she still wasn't convinced he wanted his wife in his bed.

Dully, she congratulated herself on being as logical as Nick. If she couldn't sleep with him, she'd have to keep pushing him away and walk the line between friendship and desire. She was tired of fighting. So, she chose honesty with a twist. Just like a hot toddy—the medicine went down better with a little bit of liquor.

"Nick, I'm sorry." She pulled herself to full height and wrapped herself in an invisible cloud of dignity. "I was wrong to hide those dogs from you. I'll get everything cleaned up and drive them back to the shelter in the morning. If they need me again, I'll tell you and I'm sure we can work it out."

"Alexa—"

She continued in a rush. "And about what happened here. It's okay. I got caught up in the moment like you, and I've heard anger usually turns to passion, and let's face it, we're both sexually frustrated. These episodes are bound to happen. And I don't want to talk about it—I'm sick of talking this business relationship to death. It's just about money, so we need to stick to the contract. Okay?"

. . .

Nick struggled for composure at his wife's speech. The itch between his shoulder blades warned him she hid a lot more than she let on. He knew this moment could turn on a quarter and not a dime if he took one step away from his logically plotted course.

He pushed the nagging thought away and looked at her. As the days had passed, he realized she became more beautiful to him. Light shimmered from her eyes, and her smile, and her very heart. Their dialogues pushed open doors he thought had been locked, but the result was a strange flow of emotion he didn't feel comfortable with—and never would. She was a woman who needed a secure relationship. Hell, she was a woman who deserved it. He could only give her sex and friendship. Not love.

He'd made his decision years ago. The cost was too great.

So, Nick watched the fragile thread snap between them again with a mixture of emotions and too much damn regret.

He forced a nod and a slight smile. "Apology and explanation accepted. No more analyzing."

She smiled back but her eyes remained distant. "Good. Why don't you go upstairs while I clean up?"

"I'll help."

"I'd rather do it myself."

He moved toward the stairs and studied the hound dog crouched in the corner. A long yellow body. Ugly face. Canine eyes echoed his own past—lots of pain and no one to count on. Matted fur matched a long tail hanging limply to one side. Definitely a loner, like an older kid in an orphanage flung amidst cute little babies. Probably caught trying to steal some food. Probably no family or kids or connections. The dog stood quietly at the foot of the stairs and watched him climb.

Nick remembered the summer he'd found an old mutt in

the woods. The dog was starved, with clumpy fur and hopeless eyes. Nick dragged him home and plied him with food and water. Eventually he nursed him back to health and made a friend.

He'd managed to hide him from his mother for a while, since the house was so big, and the housekeeper agreed to keep the secret. Then one day he arrived home from school and went looking for him and noticed his father was back from a trip to the Cayman Islands. He knew immediately his dog was not there. When he confronted his father, Jed Ryan laughed and gave him a rough push. "No losers in this house, buddy. Maybe if you got a real dog like a German shepherd. That mutt was good for nothing and actually crapped in the house. I got rid of it."

Jed Ryan had walked away, and Nick remem-bered the lesson again. Never get attached. He'd thought about that dog every day for years, then finally locked it away where the thought could never bother him again.

Until now.

For the second time that night, Nick hesitated, wanting to take a chance on something but too afraid of the consequences. His heart hitched with longing, unrest, confusion. Then he turned his back on his wife and the ugly dog and shut the door behind him.

Chapter Eight

Nick stood on the dock and watched the line of boats bob in the water. Cranky waves rose and hit the shore as a harbinger of winter. The burned-orange sunset cut through the threatening dark and illuminated the archway of lights from the Newburgh–Beacon Bridge. He stuck his hands in his Armani suit jacket and breathed in the fresh, clean air. Calmness seeped through his body as he stared at his beloved mountains, and once again, he knew this was where he belonged.

Ten years ago, the waterfront property had been infested with drug dealers and crack addicts. The beautiful lines of the river were steeped in garbage and the elegant brick buildings stood empty, their broken windows a cry for help. Eventually, investors saw the potential of the area and began to throw money into a dream of restoration.

Nick and his uncle had watched the project carefully

and bided their time. Somehow, they had both suspected the opportunity would finally come for Dreamscape to profit locally. The first daring person to open a bar in the area began to draw a new crowd who wanted to have a beer and some buffalo wings while watching the seagulls. As the cops descended into the heart of the city, cleanup projects sprouted from not-for-profit organizations. The last five years proved the project was worthy of investors' attention. The restaurants and spa Nick wanted to build would change the Hudson Valley forever. And he knew he was the one meant to build it.

His mind flashed back to his meeting with Hyoshi Komo. Nick had finally closed the deal. There was only one man left who stood in the way of his dream.

Michael Conte.

Nick swore softly as he watched the sun begin to sink. Hyoshi had agreed to give Nick the contract only if Michael Conte backed him. If Nick couldn't convince Conte he was the man for the job, Hyoshi would pick another architect and Dreamscape wouldn't have a chance.

Nick couldn't let that happen.

He was a man who had traveled widely in search of an education for architecture. He'd looked upon the glittering gold domes in Florence and the tall elegant towers in Paris. He'd seen pristine exotic islands; the majestic Swiss Alps; and the raw, carved rocks of the Grand Canyon.

Nothing in his sight or mind or heart came close to his mountains.

A mocking smile touched his lips as the corny thought caught and held.

He studied the view for a long time as his mind sorted his problems with his wife and the contract and Conte and still came up empty. His cell phone rang and interrupted his thoughts.

He punched the button without checking caller ID. "Hello."

"Nicky?"

He smothered a curse. "Gabriella. What do you want?"

She paused. "I need to see you. There's something important to discuss and I can't over the phone."

"I'm down by the river. Why don't you come to the office tomorrow?"

"By the marina?"

"Yes, but—"

"I'm on my way. Be there in ten."

The phone clicked.

"Son of a bitch," he muttered. He quickly went over the options and reminded himself he had every right to leave. Then the guilt pricked. Gabriella may still be upset he'd ended the relationship so abruptly. Maybe she needed to yell at him some more. He knew women believed in closure and had a thing about competition. She was probably driving herself crazy that Alexa had "won" him.

So he decided to wait and listen to her ranting, then apologize and get on with his life. Fifteen minutes later, Gabriella showed up.

He watched her climb out of her silver Mercedes convertible. She walked over with a lazy confidence that invited men to look their fill. He neutrally admired the cropped black T-shirt that exposed her flat stomach and showed off her belly ring. Hip-hugger jeans slung low, cinched with a thin black belt. Low-heeled black boots crunched on the gravel until she stopped in front of him. Wine-red lips pursed in a professional pout.

"Nick." Her eyes burned but her tone was chilly. "It's good to see you."

He nodded. "What's going on?"

"I need some advice. I got a contract offer for Lace Cosmetics."

"That's a huge account, Gabby. Congratulations. What's the problem?"

She leaned in. The expensive scent of Chanel drifted in the air. "It's a two-year deal but I'd need to relocate to California." Emerald eyes widened with the perfect amount of innocence and desire. "This is my home. And I hate *Baywatch* mentality. I've always been a die-hard New Yorker. Like you."

A warning bell clanged somewhere in his brain. "You need to decide this for yourself. It's over between us. I'm married."

"We had something real. I think you got spooked and jumped at the first female you could control."

He shook his head with a twinge of sadness. "I'm sorry, but that's not true. I have to go."

"Wait!" One moment she stood a few inches away, the next she was squished against his chest with her arms looped around his neck and her hips seriously grinding against his.

Jesus...

"I miss this," she murmured. "You know how good we are together. Marriage or no marriage, I still want you. And you want me."

"Gabriella—"

"I'll prove it." She dragged his head down to meet hers and he had a second to decide what the hell he'd do. Push her away and keep to the letter of the contract? Or take the opportunity to test the hold his wife had on him?

The thought of Alexa drifted past. He stiffened his shoulders and began to back away, but the taunting inner demon rose up and whispered its warning. His wife wasn't real, just a fleeting image that would shatter into heartbreak and pain and remind him nothing lasted. Gabriella would make him forget. Gabriella would make him remember. Gabriella would force him to face the truth of his marriage.

The truth they had no real marriage.

So, he grabbed the opportunity and took her lips, plundering her mouth as he had in the past. Her taste invaded his mouth, and her hands frantically rubbed up and down his back in an invitation to drag her to the car and take her right there, and for a little while he'd be clear of his frustration and longing for someone else.

He almost bent to her will, but then another realization took hold.

He was on automatic. Once, he'd experienced arousal with this woman. Now, there was only a minor buzz, which paled to the earth-shattering reaction Alexa caused with just a touch. Gabby's taste didn't please him, and her breasts didn't spill over into his hands, and her hips were too sharp and jabbed against his waist.

And he realized she wasn't Alexa, would never be Alexa, and he didn't want to settle.

Nick pulled away.

She took a while to accept his rejection. Sheer rage swept over her face before she managed to calm herself. He tried to stumble out an apology but she cut him off. "Something's going on, Nick. All the pieces don't add up." Her spine straightened with a stiff dignity. Nick knew every action was calculated to cause the most dramatic effect. It was another element so different between her and Alexa. "Let me tell you my theory. You needed to get married fast for some business deal and she fit the bill."

Gabriella laughed when she saw the surprised look on his face. "She's playing you, Nick. You'll never get out of this marriage without a baby or giving up a hell of a lot of money, no matter what she's told you. Your worst nightmare will come true." Her lips twisted in disgust. "Just mark my words when her little, 'Ooops, I guess we made a mistake' pops up."

Gabriella walked away and stopped with her hand on the door handle. "Good luck. I'm going to take the job in California, but if you need me, call."

She slid into the car and drove off. His spine tingled with icy foreboding. He'd bet his life Alexa could be trusted and would never try to trap him for more money—who marries a billionaire and asks for only one hundred fifty grand? Gabriella was only pissed because she hadn't been able to keep him.

Nick winced when he thought of the kiss. His first instinct was to ignore the whole episode. But he owed his wife honesty. He'd explain he and Gabriella met by the river in public, she had initiated the kiss, and now would be moving to California.

End of story. He'd be calm and rational. Alexa had no reason to be jealous. She may be a little annoyed, but a kiss was easily dismissed.

At least, that kiss was.

Some others were harder to forget.

With that thought, he walked to the car and drove home.

. . .

Alexa closed her eyes and fought a bone-weary despair.

She sat in her battered yellow Volkswagen with the windows rolled up and Prince blasting on her stereo. The bank parking lot emptied as five minutes turned into an hour and continued ticking. She stared out her windshield and tried to fight off the bitter taste of failure and disappointment that ate at her gut like acid.

No loan.

Again.

Yes, BookCrazy was doing well and she'd just turned a profit. But the bank was not thrilled with the idea of pouring more money into her business, when she barely broke even now and had no collateral and no savings and nothing to back her up. She thought of her favorite *Sex and the City* episode and wondered how many pairs of shoes she had. Then realized she didn't even have that many.

Of course, her Mr. Big was really her husband and with just a tiny addition on those loan papers she would have scored. She wondered if she'd been stupid and prideful not to use the connection, and she almost got out of the car.

Almost.

She let out a long, sorrowful groan. A deal was a deal, and she'd already collected her money. Now she was back to square one, stuck with a husband for a year who didn't like her—but who occasionally wanted to have sex until his mind cleared.

And she was dead broke.

Oh, yeah, she'd hit the jackpot.

Cursing, she started the engine and shoved the formal rejection letter into her glove compartment. Bottom line remained. She wouldn't use Nick's money to further her career when their relationship was only temporary. She needed to secure that loan on her own damn credentials. If she used Nick, the café wouldn't truly belong to her. No, she'd wait another year, garner more profits, and try again. No need to turn suicidal and depressed because of a little setback.

Guilt gnawed at her stomach. The lies added up to an impressive pile. First to her parents. Then to Nick. How was she supposed to explain the lack of expansion when Nick had already handed over the check? And her parents thought she was now rolling in dough. They'd be questioning Nick about when he'd begin the architectural work for BookCrazy. After all, why wouldn't her husband help his own wife with her business?

The elaborate tower of cards swayed and threat-ened to topple.

She drove home amidst the edges of gloom and pulled in next to Nick's car. She hoped he had made dinner, then realized she couldn't have anything but a salad because she'd cheated on her diet at lunch with a delicious, greasy cheeseburger deluxe and large fries.

Her mood turned blacker.

When she walked in, the house practically expanded with the scent of garlic and herbs and tomatoes. Alexa threw her purse on the couch, kicked off her shoes, and hiked up her skirt to rip off her pantyhose before entering the kitchen.

"What are you doing?"

He turned his head. "Making dinner."

She gave him a scowl. "I just want a salad."

"I already made it. In the refrigerator, chilling. How was your day?"

His nice tone ruffled her nerves. "Just ducky."

"That good, hmmm?"

She ignored him and poured herself a large glass of water. Water and dry lettuce complemented each other nicely. "Did you feed the fish?"

He stirred a pot of sauce that bubbled over, and the smell made saliva pool in her mouth. How the hell he had learned to cook like an old Italian grandmother was beyond her, but the whole thing was getting annoying. What husband got home from work and cooked a gourmet meal for God's sakes? He wasn't *normal*.

He threw in the spaghetti. "Odd choice of a word, isn't it? Fish is either singular or plural. Imagine my surprise when I walked into the study and found not one fish in a tiny fish bowl, but an entire aquarium."

She practically vibrated with the need to fight. "Otto was

lonely and you were practicing animal cruelty. He was too isolated. Now, he has friends and a place to swim."

"Yes, nice little tunnels and rocks and algae to play hide-and-seek with his buddies."

"You're being sarcastic."

"And you're cranky."

She slammed her water glass down on the table. Liquid sloshed over the rim. With a defiant turn on her heel, she ditched the water, walked over to the liquor cabinet, and poured herself two fingers of Scotch. The liquid sizzled down her throat and calmed her nerves. She caught sight of his shoulders shaking a little but when she looked at him with suspicion, he didn't seem to be laughing at her.

"I had a bad day."

"Wanna talk about it?"

"No. And I'm not eating any spaghetti."

"Okay."

He left her in silence while she had another drink and started to settle. She sat in the cozy kitchen surrounded by the sounds of old-fashioned cooking and a heavenly silence. He wore an apron tonight over his faded jeans and T-shirt. His grace and ease in such a domestic environment made her breath hitch just a bit.

He set the table, dispersed his food and her salad, and began to eat. Her curiosity about his day piqued.

"How's the waterfront contract going?"

He expertly rolled his spaghetti over his fork and popped it neatly into his mouth. "Had a drink with Hyoshi and he gave me his vote."

A deep sense of pleasure cut through her fog. "Nick, that's wonderful. That only leaves Michael."

He frowned. "Yeah. Conte may cause a problem."

"You can talk to him Saturday night."

His frown deepened. "I'd rather not go to the party."

"Oh. Okay, I'll go alone."

"Forget it, I'll go."

"We'll have fun. It will give you another chance to pitch him in a relaxed environment." She left her salad in front of her and stared hungrily at the bowl of spaghetti. Maybe she'd sneak in a forkful. After all, she had to try the sauce.

"If Conte nixes the deal, the whole thing is off."

"He won't."

"How do you know?"

"Because you're the best."

She concentrated on her pasta. When she finally looked up, it was to see a strange expression cross his face. He seemed unsettled. "How would you know?"

Alexa smiled. "I've seen your work. I used to watch when we were young, and you'd build things in the garage. I always thought you'd be a carpenter, but when I saw Mt. Vesuvius restaurant, I knew you found your true calling. The whole place pulled at me, Nick. From the trickling water, to the flowers and bamboo, and the resemblance to an old Japanese hut in the mountains. You're a brilliant architect."

He looked positively awestruck at her comment. Didn't he know she had always admired his talent, even when they'd ruthlessly teased each other? Even after the long years apart? "Why do you look so surprised?"

He seemed to shake off the spell. "I don't know. I never had a woman interested in my career. No one really understands it."

"Then they're stupid. Can I finish this last portion or do you want some more?"

His lips twitched as he handed over the bowl. "Be my guest." She fought a groan as the spicy tomato sauce danced on her tongue. "Alexa, what's going on with your bookstore expansion?"

The strand of spaghetti caught in her throat and she choked. He flew up from the chair and began pounding on her back, but she shook him off and guzzled a few mouthfuls of water. The poem flashed in mocking horror past her vision. *Oh, what a tangled web we weave, when first we practice to deceive...*

"Are you okay?"

"Fine. Just went down the wrong pipe." She changed the subject. "We have to go over to my parents' for Thanksgiving."

"No, I hate holidays. You didn't answer my question. You got the cash and I was under the impression you needed to start the café right away. I have some ideas I'd like to go over with you."

Her heart beat so fast the blood roared in her head. This was bad. Very, very bad. "Umm, Nick, I don't expect you to help me with the café. You have enough on your plate with the waterfront project and the board hounding your every step. Besides, I already sort of hired someone."

"Who?"

Shit.

She waved her hand in the air in a dismissive gesture. "Forgot his name. A customer recommended him. He's, um, drawing up the plans and we'll start soon. I may wait until spring."

He frowned. "No reason to wait. I don't trust this guy already. Give me his number and I'll talk to him."

"No."

"Why not?"

"Because I don't want you involved." The words seemed to punch him like a surprise right hook. He winced, then quickly recovered. The misery of her lies festered, but she reminded herself to stick to business, even though she knew in some strange way she'd hurt him.

His face reflected disinterest. "Fine. If that's what you prefer."

Her voice gentled. "I'd just like to stick to business in our relationship. Getting you involved in my café project isn't a good idea. Don't you agree?"

"Sure. Whatever you want."

The silence beat around them and verged on awkwardness. She cleared her throat. "Back to Thanksgiving. You have to go; there's no choice."

"Tell them I have to work."

"You're going. It's important to my family. They'd suspect something's up if we don't attend."

"I hate Thanksgiving."

"I heard you the first time but I still don't care."

"Family holidays weren't in the contract."

"Sometimes we can't follow the contract to the letter."

His head popped up from his plate like she suddenly had his full attention. "You're probably right. We have to allow for some flexibility and maybe some mistakes along the way."

She nodded and forked in the last mouthful. "Exactly. So, you'll come?"

"Sure."

His total turnaround made her pause, but she ignored it. Her empty bowl mocked her. Damn, what had she done?

"Funny you mentioned the contract," he said. "A little problem came up but it's solved now."

Maybe she'd do some extra work on the treadmill. And lift some weights. Maybe even go back to yoga class.

"I wasn't going to say anything but I wanted to be honest. You probably won't even care."

She'd call Maggie tomorrow and go to kickboxing. The class burned more calories and was good for self-defense.

"Gabriella kissed me."

Her head shot up. "What did you say?"

He shrugged. "She called and wanted to meet me. She said she's moving to California. I didn't initiate, so I guess it was her idea of a good-bye kiss. End of story."

Her eyes narrowed. His seemingly casual attitude masked a deeper truth. She also knew the way to get it was to play the whole thing off.

"A good-bye kiss, huh? Well, that doesn't sound too threatening." She watched him practically slump in the chair with relief. She pretended to be engaged with the leftover leaves from her salad to take the pressure off. "Cheek or lips?"

"Lips. Quick, though."

"Okay. So no tongue, right?"

The chair squeaked with his definite squirm. The son of a bitch was busted. "Not really."

"Sure?"

"Maybe a little. Happened so fast I don't remember."

Even when they were kids, he'd sucked at lying. He got in trouble every time and Maggie escaped punishment because she was damn good. Nick's nose practically grew and screamed the truth to the world.

"Okay. The main thing is you told me the truth. Where did this happen?"

"Down by the river."

"After your meeting?"

"Yep."

"She called on your cell phone."

"I told her not to come but she said it was important so I waited for her. I told her I wanted nothing more to do with her."

"Then she kissed you and you pushed her away."

"Right."

"Where were her hands?"

Confusion muddied his features. He seemed to think it over as if afraid it was a trick question. "What do you mean?"

"Her hands. Around your neck, waist, where?"

"Around my neck."

"Where were your hands?"

"Before or after I pushed her away?"

Bingo.

"Before."

"Around her waist."

"Okay. So it sounds like it was a while before you finally pushed her away, and tongue was involved, and her body was plastered to yours for about how long?"

He looked at her empty Scotch glass with lust but answered the question. "Not long."

"One minute? A second?"

"A couple of minutes. Then I pushed her away."

"Yes, you said that already."

She got up from the table and started clearing the dishes. He hesitated as if unsure what to do, but he remained seated. An awkward silence descended. Alexa finished the task without speaking and let the tension build. She almost heard the visible snap as he broke.

"You have no reason to be upset."

She stacked the dishes in the washer, then turned her attention back to the refrigerator. With methodical motions, she took out the ice cream, chocolate syrup, whipped cream, and cherries.

"Why would I be upset? The kiss was nothing, even if you did break the contract."

"We just said that sometimes the contract can't be followed to the letter. What are you doing?"

"Making dessert. So, what did Gabriella do when you pushed her away?"

She continued creating the perfect sundae and let him dangle in discomfort. "She was upset because I rejected her."

"Why'd you push her away, Nick?"

He looked distinctly uncomfortable. "Because we made

some promises. Even if we're not sleeping together, we agreed I wouldn't cheat."

"Very logical. I'm surprised you were able to think so clearly after such a kiss. With me, I understand. But Gabriella seems to inspire a more passionate response."

His mouth dropped open. She swished the whipped cream and drizzled a few cherries on top, then stood back to admire her creation.

"You think I react more passionately to Gabriella?"

She lifted one shoulder. "It was obvious the night I met her you two tore up the sheets together. We don't have that problem. The only times you've ever kissed me were when you were pissed off or bored."

"Bored?" He rubbed his face with his hands and tore his fingers through his hair. A humorless laugh escaped his lips. "I don't believe this. You have no idea how I was feeling when Gabriella kissed me."

A sliver of ice pierced her heart, as precise as a surgeon's scalpel. This time there was no bleeding, just a numb acceptance the man she married would always lust after a supermodel and not her. He'd always be weak enough to grab one last taste before his damn ethics took over. He was legally faithful, but mentally a cheater.

She was an afterthought and he'd never want her as completely as his ex. At least, not physically.

The anger took hold, fierce and satisfying, as she stared at her perfect chocolate sundae. Nicholas Ryan worshipped logic and reason and had carefully thought through her response. He used honesty because he was a fair man. What enraged her was his incapability of seeing her for a woman who had every right to be pissed off when she found out her husband kissed his ex-lover. He expected her to be calm, civil, politely forgive his indiscretion, and move on.

Screw him.

With one graceful motion, she lifted the heavy, dripping bowl, and dumped it on top of his head.

He let out a yelp and leaped up, knocking the chair over, his face registering pure disbelief as chocolate ice cream and syrup and cream dripped over his head, slid down his cheeks, and tunneled into his ears.

"What the hell?" His roar was filled with confusion and irritation and an honest emotion that made her feel immediately better.

With satisfaction, she wiped her sticky hands on the dishtowel and stepped back. She even managed a pleasant smile. "Being the clearheaded, reasonable man you're supposed to be, you should have pushed Gabriella away and honored the contract. Instead, you made out with her in public, at the river, with your tongue in her mouth and your hands on her body. This is my clearheaded, reasonable response to your betrayal, you son of a bitch. Enjoy your dessert."

She turned on her heel and walked up the stairs.

· · ·

A week later, Nick watched his wife work the room and admitted he'd made a mistake.

Big time.

If he were a lesser man, he'd wish to be taken back in time and reenact the scene with Gabriella and the kiss. He'd push her away, proudly tell his wife of his actions, and enjoy a different result. Since he despised such weak-hearted desires, there was only one recourse left.

Suffer.

Alexa walked amongst the guests like a glittering peacock, dressed in bold scarlet instead of the sophisticated black the elite crowd favored. Her hair was pinned up with loose curls left to fall free around her neck and shoulders.

She practically dared him to say something when she appeared at the foot of the stairs, but this time he kept his mouth shut, commented politely on how nice she looked, and escorted her into the car. The whole episode was accompanied by the cold silence that had drifted into a full week.

Aggravation ripped through him. She'd been the one to dump a bowl of ice cream on him. Did she apologize? No. Just treated him with a neutral cordiality that made him nuts. She stayed out of his way, kept to her bedroom, and remained quiet at dinner.

Nick didn't want to know why her distance made him want to grab her and force her to show some emotion. He didn't want to analyze the loneliness eating at his insides, or why he missed their chess games or their fights or just hanging around with her in the evening. He missed the annoying calls at work regarding Otto or begging him to adopt a dog from her shelter.

Instead, he had what he'd wanted in the first place.

A wife in name only. A business partner who kept to herself and led her own life.

He hated it.

The memory of their last kiss flashed before his vision. But her words puzzled him. Didn't she realize how much he ached for her?

He'd thought the night the police arrived had proven his interest. Instead, she'd thrown Gabriella out as proof he could never desire her in the same way. God help him, he'd never wanted Gabriella the way he wanted his wife. Never dreamed about Gabriella or ached to touch her or laugh with her. Never wanted to fight or play stupid games or have a life with Gabriella.

What was happening to him?

Nick drained his glass and moved across the room.

Maybe it was time to find out.

• • •

"Husband alert."

Alexa looked up and saw Nick cut away from the crowd. She ignored him and focused her attention on Michael and the amusement that glinted in his eyes. She wagged her finger at her new friend. "Behave."

"Don't I always, *cara*?"

"This is the second time tonight you've kept me from my husband."

Their heels clicked on the polished wood floors as he led her toward the back study. His home was decorated in rich earth and burgundy tones, with touches of gilded mirrors, tapestries, and smooth marble sculptures to break up the flow of polished elegance that permeated the rooms. Opera played on the stereo system piped throughout the floors. Michael had decorated with an underlying sensuality Alexa appreciated.

"Then I am doing my job well, *signora*. He makes you sad tonight, I can tell."

She paused and looked up at him. For the first time, she allowed the raw emotion of Nick's confession to escape. It had been difficult pretending not to care this past week. "We had a fight."

"Do you want to tell me about it?"

"Men suck."

He nodded with a flourish. "Sometimes, yes. Sometimes when we wear our hearts on our sleeves, we are wonderful. But mostly we are scared of breaking open ourselves to another."

"Some men never do."

"Yes. Some never do. You must keep trying."

She smiled at him. "I'm giving you my friend Maggie's number. Promise me you'll call her."

He gave a long sigh. "If this will make you happy, I shall call her and invite her to dinner."

"*Grazie*. I just can't shake this odd instinct I have about you two."

"Ah, you are a matchmaker at heart, *cara*."

As the night wore on, she drank more champagne and spoke more boldly and danced with more partners, always careful to walk the edgy line between proper party conduct and having a good time. Soon, Nick gave up trying to engage her in private conversation. He just stood by the bar, drinking

Scotch and staring. His gaze burned into her from across the room, even when hiding behind the barriers of people. As if he laid claim to her, without a word or a touch. The thought made her shiver with pure anticipation. Then she realized she was actually fantasizing about Nick making a scene and dragging her off to seduce her. Like in one of her romance novels.

Sure. Mr. Logical himself. Might as well read science fiction and wait for the aliens to take over the world. That was much more likely.

. . .

He'd had enough.

Nick was sick and tired of watching her parade around with various men. Sure, she only danced with them. But she'd rarely left Conte's side, falling into an almost easy banter and level of comfort that pissed Nick off.

Their marriage was supposed to look solid to outsiders. What if the gossip windmill flew regarding the Italian count and Alexa? The waterfront contract would be even stickier, because as he negotiated, he'd fantasize about breaking Mr. Smooth's pretty-boy face.

Oh, yes, he was being logical, all right.

As Nick finished his last drink and placed the glass on the bar, he noted the fiery alcohol heated his blood with a new resolve and stripped away the barriers to the truth.

He wanted to make love to his wife.

He wanted her for real, for just a little while.

And damn the consequences.

He cut off the rational man who screamed at him to back off, wait until morning, and finish up the next months in polite civility.

He crossed the room and tapped her shoulder.

She spun around. Nick deliberately gripped her hand. Surprise flashed across her face, then smoothed away.

"Are you ready?" she asked politely.

"Yes. I think I'm ready for a lot of things."

She nibbled at her bottom lip, probably wondering if he was drunk. He took the matter under his control to separate Michael from her as quickly as possible.

"Michael, I wonder if you'd be kind enough to call us a cab? I don't want to risk the drive. I'll send someone tomorrow to pick up the car."

The count nodded with graciousness. "Of course. I'll be back in a moment."

Nick kept his hand locked on Alexa's and led her over to the coatroom, determined not to let her out of his sight. In a few hours, she'd be in the only place where she couldn't get in any trouble. And it wasn't over any rainbow.

It was in his bed.

She didn't seem to notice anything had changed between them. Nick watched while she slipped on her coat and said good-bye to her new friends. He was amazed she didn't suspect tonight was her official wedding night. The secret knowledge made him even more impatient to get out of Conte's house, where he'd finally seduce her. He'd been crazy to wait this long. He should have known sex was the fastest way to ensure a relationship settled.

The cab arrived and they sped home. She remained silent at his side, stared out the window, and ignored him.

He paid the driver and followed her inside. She hung her coat neatly in the closet and headed up the stairs. "Good night."

He knew anger was the quickest way to gain her full attention. "Alexa?"

"Yes?"

"Did you sleep with him?"

Her head spun halfway around, reminding him of the little girl from *The Exorcist*. Her mouth dropped open and a gasp rose to her lips. Fierce satisfaction ripped through him at her response, and the connection between them reignited and caught fire.

"What did you say?"

He took off his own jacket and threw it over the back of the couch. He stood in front of her, hands on hips, and gathered all his power to make her mad as hell. Because he knew through her anger he'd find honesty—the passionate woman she hid from him in her ridiculous belief he didn't want her.

"You heard me the first time. I wondered if you had time to make it to the bedroom or did Conte just take you against the wall before dessert?"

She ripped in her breath and clenched her fingers into tight fists. "I don't screw other men or kiss them in public because I have more respect for our marriage than you do. And so does Michael."

Her immediate defense of Conte made a tight ball of

rage twist in the pit of his stomach like a bunch of poisonous snakes. "You let him paw you in front of my business associates."

"You're nuts! He was a perfect gentleman. Besides, you were all over Gabriella in a public parking lot!"

"That was different. I pushed her away."

"Sure, after you stuck your tongue in her mouth. I'm done here."

His eyes narrowed into slits. "Not yet."

She blinked and stepped back. Then looked straight into his eyes and cracked the final whip. "I'm going to bed. You may be able to control who I don't sleep with, but you don't have any power over my fantasies."

Her icy tone contradicted the mocking words pulsing in the air between them.

He broke.

Nick walked toward her with a steady slowness that made her move away for every footstep forward. Her back slammed against the wall when he reached her. Slowly, he splayed his palms flat against the wall on either side of her head. His body caged hers. His wide stance trapped her between his legs.

He bent over and directed his words right against her lips. "If you want sex so badly, all you have to do is ask."

Her entire body stiffened. "I'm not interested in you." The wildly beating pulse at her neck contradicted her words.

"Try again."

"Go play your head games with Gabriella."

"You want me. Why don't you finally admit it?"

Fury spat from her in waves. "I don't want you. I just want your money."

He realized her ploy had worked before, but tonight he didn't care.

He closed the distance another tight inch. Her breasts pressed against his chest, and her nipples were hard little points stabbing out of the scarlet material, begging to be freed. Her breath came in ragged gasps, her perfume swamped his senses. He grew hard, and her eyes widened as his full length throbbed against her leg in demand.

"I'm calling your bluff, baby."

Pure shock registered on her face as he removed one hand from the wall to casually unbutton his shirt, slide off his tie, then grasp her chin with a firm grip.

"Prove it."

He stamped his mouth over hers, not giving her a chance to think or back off or push him away. He invaded her mouth, plunging his tongue inside the slick, silky cave, then closed his lips around the wet flesh and sucked hard.

She grabbed for his shoulders and made a little moan deep in her throat.

Then she exploded.

. . .

Alexa reached up and tangled her fingers into his hair, holding his head as she kissed him back and met demand with demand. Her hips rose up to thrust against him, and his taste and smell invaded her like a drug.

Her skin burned as all the pent-up desire she'd buried deep burst out of her body in a flood of heat. She was ravenous for his taste, for his hands to strip off her clothes and take her right there against the wall, and she reveled in his wild response that was so opposite his rigid control.

Control.

An alarm bell rang in her head and cut through the mist of sexual fog. He'd been drinking. If they were interrupted, he might calmly step away with a reasonable explanation as to why sex would not be a good idea.

The knowledge he'd done it twice before skated along the edges of her mind, until she dragged her mouth from his and yanked the hair at the nape of his neck.

His head shot up. He blinked as if coming to from a long sleep, and she caught the question held in his eyes. Alexa made herself say the one thing she didn't want to say.

"I don't think this is a good idea."

She held her breath and waited for him to step back, waited for the fog to clear from his mind, waited for him to agree. She got her second shock of the night when he smiled down at her—a dangerous, masculine smile that promised unspoken pleasures and raw, hungry sex.

"I don't care."

He easily tossed her over his shoulder as if she were a china doll instead of an Amazon. With an easy grace, he climbed the stairs and headed straight for her room. Her breasts bounced against his back and her belly was crushed against the hard bone of his shoulder, but she couldn't dredge up any words to inform him this was ancient caveman behavior and no longer acceptable.

Because Alexa loved every moment.

He tossed her on the bed and finished his strip tease. Unbuttoned his shirt and threw it on the floor. Slid the belt buckle from the loops and lowered the zipper. Kicked off his pants in one swift motion. All of this was done as she sprawled in the center of the bed and stared at him as if he were her own private Chippendales dancer.

Nope, he was even better.

All lean sinewy muscle and gilded blond hair. Trim hips and hard thighs and an erection that stood proudly between his legs, hidden from view by a pair of black briefs. Her fingers curled into her palms as her fantasy joined her on the bed and settled against her.

"Your turn." His voice scraped like sandpaper over her ears, one side rough, the other smooth. He reached behind her and slid the zipper down. Her muscles trembled as his hands settled over the spaghetti straps of her dress and stopped. Her breath hitched as seconds beat past, and the heavy weight of his palm pressed against the top of her breasts. Her heart pounded so loud she knew he heard it. Anticipation cranked hard between them until she battled a scream, and then he hooked his index finger underneath the strap and pulled it down.

Oh, God.

Cool air rushed over her skin, but his gaze scorched as he drank in the flesh revealed. Her nipples hardened into points as the silk caught briefly, then continued on its path. He gently maneuvered her arms out of the holes, then moved the fabric even lower, exposing her belly and hips. He stopped and studied every inch of her nakedness with a silent intensity that unnerved her, until she longed to say something but the words died in her throat.

His hands settled on her hips. He grasped the delicate fabric at both sides and began to work it down over her thighs, calves, then tore it away from her sandals and tossed the dress to the floor.

Their breaths rose and fell together in an uneven, choppy rhythm. Liquid heat pulsed and pounded between her thighs, masked by the scrap of red panties she had pulled on with no one in mind but herself. But now Nick focused his attention in that direction, still saying nothing, studying the apex of her thighs, his thumb lightly brushing the line of her panties as she sucked in her breath and waited. As if he had all the time in the world, he began to play with the elastic band as if testing its strength. Alexa's entire focus shrank to those five fingers and the slow torture they bestowed. He explored the crease at her thighs, then traced an invisible line down the center of her body. He watched every reaction in silence, as if she were his love slave and he was a king used to obedience.

She exploded with sheer frustration.

"Damn it, are you going to sit there and look at me all night or are you going to *do* something?"

He gave a low chuckle. That full lower lip twitched. He hooked one leg around hers and moved over her in one quick motion. Hip to hip, thigh to thigh. Every muscle pressed against hers. Each delicious inch of his arousal cradled between her legs. He worked the pins from her hair and combed through the strands so the waves tumbled over her shoulders. Then he dipped his mouth and nipped at her earlobe, teased the tip of his tongue against the delicate shell of her ear, then blew out a warm stream of breath.

She jumped.

He laughed and whispered against her temple. "I intend on doing something. I've thought about looking at you for so long, I figured I'd indulge. But it looks like you also have a temper in bed, so I'll move it along."

"Nick—"

"Not now, Alexa. I'm busy."

He covered her lips with his and plunged his tongue deep into her mouth. She arched like a bow as the lightning crack of energy ripped through her. Her fingers clung to him as she held on and kissed him back, drowning in the taste of Scotch and male heat. He parted her legs and tortured her with promises of his hands and his penis, until she became crazed with need, until there was no more pride or logic, just this ache to have him inside her.

His mouth moved on her breasts, sucked her nipples, and nipped with his teeth. His fingers stroked her belly and hips and hooked under the lace to play, one long index finger moving underneath to test her heat, drenched with moisture as she cried out for more, always more.

He slid off her panties and plunged a finger deep inside, then added another, rubbing delicately over the hard nub hidden between curls, just giving her a taste of it until...

She cried out and her hips bucked as the climax took her

hard. Her body shook with pleasure as he shed his briefs and covered himself with a condom. He slid back up her silken length, interlaced all ten fingers with hers, and pressed their joined hands deep into the pillows.

Alexa blinked, dazed by the endless depths of his eyes, a deep, dark brown that held an array of secrets and a gleam of tenderness she'd never seen before.

He pressed against her, seeking entry. Liquid warmth rushed out to ease his welcome and she lifted her hips to take him. He pressed an inch, then another. Her body tightened around him and she panicked, knowing she'd finally belong to him, knowing he'd never want her in the way she needed.

He paused, almost as if he sensed her emotions. "Too fast? Talk to me."

She shuddered with pure need as she felt him retreat one precious inch. "No, I just, I need—"

"Tell me."

A fine sheen of tears filmed over, her emotions raw and easy for him to read. "I need you to want me. Only me. Not—"

"Oh, Jesus." He closed his eyes. Alexa watched sheer agony ripple over his face. He stopped at her entrance and bent to kiss her.

He tenderly mated his tongue with hers, stroking, tracing the swollen flesh of her lips in an action that bespoke pure humbleness. And when he opened his eyes and looked into hers, she sucked in her breath as he finally let her in, let her see it all, and gave her what she needed.

The truth.

"It's always been you. I don't want anybody else; I don't dream about anybody else. It's only you."

She cried out as he buried himself to the hilt inside of her. Her body opened and accepted his swollen length, hugged him deep and demanded more. His fingers gripped hers and pressed harder into the pillow as he began to move, slowly at first, joining her to the rhythm. She climbed again with him, and the twisting spiral path tensed her muscles, stopped her breath, and teased her with each inch as she moved closer to release.

It was a raw combining of needs, rough and primitive, and she reveled in the honesty of their lovemaking as sweat slid down his forehead and her nails dug deep into his back until she exploded. Pleasure broke over in waves, and she heard him cry out as he joined her, and in that moment they were one.

He rolled so she sprawled on top of him, her cheek against his slick muscled chest, her hair spilling over her face, her arms wrapped around his waist. No thoughts claimed her in this moment, and she treasured the deep peace as she let herself go, safe in his embrace. She slid toward sleep as he held her tightly.

. . .

Nick inched out of bed, careful not to wake his wife, and padded naked out of her room to search for some clothes. He threw on a Yankees T-shirt, remembered their deal, and exchanged it for a plain black tank with a pair of sweatpants. His lips curved as he remembered her glee when the Yanks failed in the playoffs. He went down the stairs and started the coffee, pausing to watch the sun struggle up over the mountains in the early morning light.

He considered this marriage officially consum-mated.

Nick rubbed a hand over the back of his neck and tried to think rationally. He sure hadn't thought last night. Not that he had any regrets. Surprise flickered through him at the realization. He'd wanted Alexa for a long time, and last night proved why. Everything was different with her. The way her body fit his, the way her pleasure satisfied him. He loved the way she looked into his eyes and dragged her nails over his back and experienced multiple orgasms. He loved the way she screamed his name. They had reached for each other many times through the hours, their hunger insatiable. But it wasn't just the physical that made the encounter so mind-blowing. It was the other connections, to her mind and soul. The way she let him see her vulnerability, the way she let him in when no promises had been made, no words spoken.

She scared the hell out of him.

He poured a mug of the steaming brew and took a moment in the kitchen to gather his thoughts. They needed to talk. Their relationship had reached a fork in the road, and after the last hours in her company, he didn't know if he could turn back. His original intention to avoid sex had been about avoiding emotion.

Wasn't possible anymore. He had feelings for Alexa: some desire, some friendship. Along with other elements he wasn't able to name.

At the end of the year, he still intended to walk away.

There was really no other option. A real marriage with kids wasn't in his future. But for now, they could enjoy each other instead of fighting the attraction. He was positive Alexa would be able to handle it. She knew him, knew he wasn't capable of making a true future commitment, but realized his emotions delved deeper than a casual roll in the hay.

He nodded to himself, pleased with the outcome. Yes, they'd explore this intense attraction for the upcoming months. Crazy for them not to grab the opportunity.

Satisfied with his logic, he poured his wife a cup of coffee and started up the stairs.

. . .

Alexa mushed her face deep into the pillow as the reality of the situation hit her like a freight train.

She'd slept with her husband.

Not once. Not twice. But at least three times. Too many to term it a crazy mistake. And too wildly intense to chalk it up to a one-nighter.

My God, she'd never be able to keep her hands off of him again.

She groaned and forced herself to look at the situation with some neutrality. Hard to do when her thighs ached and the scent of sex clung to the sheets. She still tasted him on her tongue, still felt the imprint of his fingers on her body. How could she possibly be expected to move on and pretend last night never mattered?

She couldn't. Therefore, she needed a new plan.

Why not keep things the way they were?

She sighed deeply and tried to analyze her emotions with the coldness of a surgeon making the first cut. Yes, the pact clearly stated no sex, but that had been to protect both of them from turning to other partners. What if they just continued as is? Could she handle it?

They wanted each other. She believed his desire for her now; his body had clearly told her what her mind denied. Last night had been much more than sex, but a strange commingling of friendship and respect and need. And...

She slammed the barrier down on *that* scary thought and moved on.

Okay, so what if she suggested they continue to sleep together until the year ended? They'd maintain their friendship and put an end to the horrible sexual tension, while enjoying each other for the next few months. Yes, her deepening feelings for him terrified her. Yes, she may get her heart broken when he walked away. But she knew him, knew he was so hung up on his rotten upbringing, no woman would earn his trust.

She didn't have false expectations.

Alexa ached to take a risk. She wanted him in her bed, wanted to take what she could for this short time and at least have the memories. She was safe because she had no illusions.

Her gut lurched at her last thought but she ignored the warning.

Then the door opened.

Nick hesitated, coffee mug in hand. A faint blush stained her cheeks at his intense stare, and she casually slid one naked leg under the barrier of the covers and rolled to her side.

"Hey."

"Hey," she repeated. An awkward silence beat around them in the typical morning-after episode. Alexa motioned toward the coffee. "For me?"

"Oh, yeah." He moved toward her and sat on the edge of the bed. The mattress dipped under his weight, and he handed her the mug, watching as she took an appreciative sniff of the rich Colombian roast. She sighed with pleasure after a taste.

"Good?"

"Perfect. I hate wimpy coffee."

His lower lip twitched. "I figured." He didn't say anything for a while as she drank. He seemed to wait for an opening, but Alexa figured he couldn't ask her if she slept well, since they had hardly closed their eyes.

His male scent rose to her nostrils like a mate seeking her own. He hadn't showered. The thin black tank left his arms and upper chest exposed, and his pants hung low on the waist, giving her a glimpse of burnished skin and a tight stomach. A raw heat tingled between her thighs and she shifted slightly on the bed. Damn if she wasn't becoming a nympho with this man. One more time and she'd need a cane to get into her bookstore, but her body didn't seem to care.

"How do you feel?" he asked.

She blinked and tilted her head upward. A lock of hair slipped over his forehead, and his jaw was darkened with stubble. She noticed he kept his attention on her face rather than the slippery sheet that kept falling down and revealing her breasts. Usually shy, a twinge of mischief danced through her with the need to test his control. She stretched in front of him to place her mug on the side table. The sheet tightened, then surrendered as she loosened her grip. The air rushed over her naked breasts and teased her nipples into tight peaks. She pretended not to notice and answered his question.

"Fine. My muscles are a bit sore, though. I need a hot shower."

"Yes, a shower."

"Do you want some breakfast?"

"Breakfast?"

"I'll cook something once I get dressed. You don't have to go into the office today, do you?"

"I don't think so."

"Okay. What do you want?"

"Want?"

"Yeah. For breakfast."

She propped her head up with one hand and studied him. He swallowed hard and tightened his jaw, as if desperately trying to pay attention to her words instead of her half-naked body.

Alexa held back a laugh and upped the ante. Her leg snaked out from underneath the covers and she stretched. She flexed and wiggled her toes in the air. Then hooked her knee over the sheet and bent it at an angle.

Nick cleared his throat. "I'm not hungry. Have to go to work."

"You said you're not working."

"Right." Her skin practically tingled under his lustful gaze.

Excitement pumped through her veins at the thought of him crawling back into bed to make love to her again, but she didn't have a clue as to how to do it.

She gathered her forces and went for the jugular. "So, are we going to talk about last night?"

He flinched, then nodded. When she remained quiet, he seemed forced to respond with something. "Last night was good."

She propped herself up. The sheet did fall and stayed put around her waist. Bare breasted, she leaned on one elbow and tossed her hair over her shoulder and out of her eyes. She ignored the strange sound he made and continued the conversation. "Just good?"

"No, no, it was great." He paused. "Really great."

The man was definitely breaking. She pressed on. "I'm glad. I've been thinking about us and where we go from here. We can move on and decide not to sleep together again. Keep things less complicated, right?"

His head bobbed up and down as he glanced at her breasts. "Right."

"Or we can continue."

"Continue?"

"To have sex."

"Mmmm."

"What do you think?"

"About what?"

Alexa wondered if his mind had fizzled or if all the blood really did leave a man's head to go somewhere else. One quick glance confirmed her suspicions. Her plan was definitely working. She just needed him to admit he wanted to keep sleeping with her and she was sure the rest would work out.

"Nick?"

"Yeah?"

"Are you going to answer the question?"

"What was the question?"

"Do we keep having sex until the marriage is over or do we go back to being just friends?"

"Alexa?"

"Yeah?"

"I vote for sex."

One moment she was enjoying this slow torture, the next he'd pinned her down, climbed on top of her naked body, and dragged her up to meet his mouth.

The kiss was a hot morning welcome. His lips devoured hers, his tongue slid inside to tease and play, then drink hungrily. He rubbed his mouth back and forth and his jawline scraped her tender flesh with his stubble. His hands pulled the sheet away from her body so he could stroke and arouse, building the heat with quick, efficient motions until a moan escaped her and she parted her thighs.

He reached for the bedside table, then paused when she stopped him.

"I'm on the pill," she murmured. "To regulate my periods."

That was all he needed. Nick yanked down his sweatpants, pressed his palms on the inside of her thighs, and surged.

She gasped. Dug her nails into his shoulders. And held on.

He punished her for teasing him, bringing her to the very edge, then backing off as she teetered on the edge of orgasm.

He dipped his head and tasted her breasts, licked her nipples, then began the climb again, only to bring her right back down. She tossed her head back and forth on the pillow, reached out, and cupped his cheeks, forcing him to look at her. His rough morning stubble scratched her skin.

"Now."

He held on with an iron-fisted control she both admired and hated. A sexy grin tugged at his lips. "Say please."

She gritted out a curse as she neared the edge again. Madness ripped through her and Alexa made a vow to never play power games with her husband again, for his retribution was too brutal. She arched her hips with fierce demand. "Please."

He plunged forward and she rocketed into her climax. Her body clenched with convulsions, and she held onto him tightly as he followed. Still inside of her, he collapsed and rested his head on the pillow beside her. Their choppy breathing filled the air.

She closed her eyes for a brief moment. The musky scent of sex and coffee mixed and rose to her nostrils. A tiny flare of fear stirred to life as she lay in his arms. After one night, her body welcomed him as her other half. Alexa wasn't one to casually dive into sexual encounters. She was the type of who fell in love, fell hard, and dreamed of happily ever after.

But there were no fairy-tale endings with Nick Ryan. He had made that clear from the first. She needed to remember his limitations every day, especially after sex. Separate the physical from the emotional. Keep her heart guarded in a tower so high and so strong, even Rapunzel would never have escaped. Enjoy her orgasms and a bit of friendship, then walk away.

Sure. No problem.

Her heart screamed *LIAR*, but she ignored it.

"I guess this cements the deal," she said.

He chuckled and threw his arm over her body. She snuggled closer. "I think we made a logical choice. Now we have something more interesting to do than chess or poker."

She bit playfully at his shoulder. "You're not getting out of our tournaments, buster. We'll just spice things up a bit."

"Such as?"

"Ever play strip poker?"

"You're an amazing woman, Alexa."

"I know."

Chapter Nine

"I don't want to go."

"I heard you the first time, the second, and the third. Now be quiet and pull in the driveway slowly. The wine will tip over."

"I hate family functions."

Alexa prayed for patience. Nick reminded her of a kid who dragged his feet and wanted to stay home to play with his toys instead of see relatives.

The past two weeks had flown past in relative smoothness except for his growing complaints regarding the holiday. Maggie had reminded her Thanksgiving with the Ryans had been more of a Halloween nightmare, so Alexa gave her husband a wide berth but refused to let him off the proverbial hook. "We don't have a choice. As a married couple, we're expected to show up for dinner. There won't be too many people there, anyway."

Nick snorted. "I'll be bored."

"Get drunk."

He scowled and swung into the driveway. The pile of cakes and pies and wine clattered in the backseat but held steady. She reached for the door handle, left the car, and stretched out her legs. The bite of November wind ripped up her skirt and through the thick tights she wore under her mini. She shivered and looked at the cars already lined up on the lawn. "I knew we'd be late."

His features changed, became softer, more intimate. Those chestnut depths gleamed with memories from early this morning, of warm, tangled sheets and cries and long wet kisses. Her body came to immediate attention. Her nipples pressed against her purple sweater, and an achy heat pooled between her thighs.

He reached over and ran one finger down her cheek, then lightly traced her lower lip. "I clearly asked if you wanted to continue, remember?"

Heat rushed to her cheeks. "You shouldn't have started in the first place. You knew we'd be late."

"We could skip the whole thing and spend Thanksgiving in bed." Her stomach dipped at his low murmur. "What do you think?"

"I think you're trying to bribe me."

"Is it working?"

"No. Let's go." She heard his low laugh behind her. He knew she lied. He always tempted her. After two weeks of steady sex, she still couldn't get enough of her husband, and a day in bed with him sounded like sheer heaven.

She carried in the pies and he grabbed the wine. The door was open and they were immediately folded into family chaos, with loud greetings and handshakes, drinks thrust into open hands, and a thousand different conversations overlapping.

"Hi, Ma." She kissed Maria and took an apprec-iative sniff of the plump turkey filled with sausage stuffing. A cloud of moist, fragrant steam rose in the air and wrapped her in warmth. "Smells great. You look pretty."

"Thanks. It's amazing what paying off the mortgage does for stress load."

Fear shot through her. She leaned in. "Mom, please don't mention it—remember our deal?"

Maria sighed. "Ok, honey. I'm just so grateful and it feels strange not to say something."

"Mom!"

"Fine, my lips are sealed." Her mom gave her a quick kiss and readied the tray of antipasto.

Alexa plucked a green olive from the tray of appetizers. "I'll bring it out."

"Don't eat them all on the way. Where's Nick?"

"Talking with Dad in the living room."

"God help us."

Alexa smiled and joined her husband. He reached for a black olive and popped it in his mouth. *Typical*, she thought. He liked black olives, she liked green. So many ways they were complete opposites. In other aspects, they were perfectly in sync.

Her niece raced down the hall. Honey blond hair tumbled around her shoulders, and her legs and feet were bare underneath her green party dress, a rich velvet with a frothy skirt that made her seem like a fairy princess. Taylor hurled herself into her arms with a leap, and Alexa caught her with ease. She slid her around to rest on one hip. "Hey, squirt."

"Aunt Al, I want ice cream."

"You can have some later."

"Okay. I want an olive."

"Green or black?"

She made a terrible face only a toddler could master. "Green is yucky."

Alexa rolled her eyes at her husband's look of triumph. Nick took a fat black olive and stuck it on the end of his finger. "The child has great taste. Here you go." He offered it up and watched her chew in delight. "Good?"

"Hmmm. Now can I have ice cream?"

Alexa laughed. "After dinner, okay? Go tell Mommy to finish dressing you."

"Okay." Taylor scurried off and left the adults together amidst drinking and munching and frequent bursts of laughter.

Alexa noted her husband took her advice and started drinking early. He held his Scotch and soda with tight fingers. He nodded at various conversations but retained an air of assessing distance that caused her heart to ache. Then his gaze broke and lifted to meet hers.

Fire.

The air lit and charged around them. He raised his brow in comic wickedness and motioned toward one of the bedrooms.

She shook her head and laughed. Then spun on her heel to go find her cousins.

...

Nick watched his wife enjoy the closeness of her family. He remembered his own holidays at home. His mother drank while his father made passes at all the other attractive female guests. He remembered being able to sneak in bottles of liquor and cigarettes because nobody cared. He remembered the overstuffed turkey for show, cooked by the maid, and the Christmas presents his parents never stayed around to watch them open.

The McKenzies seemed different. Genuine warmth beat beneath all the usual chaos. Even Jim seemed to fit in again, even though it must have taken years for Maria's sister to finally forgive him. Alexa's family may have been broken, but they had weathered the storm and now seemed even stronger.

Nick struggled to play the part of the newly married husband and not get sucked into the ruse. The tiny glow of belonging grew to a strong flare, but he snuffed it out with a decisive blow. This was not his family and he was only tolerated because he'd married Alexa. He needed to remember that. A dull ache pressed against his chest but he ignored it. Sure, they seemed to accept him, but only because they believed the marriage was real. Like all things, acceptance would end, too.

He might as well get used to the idea early.

Jim thumped him on the back and called over his brother. "Charlie, did you hear what Nick's doing down by the waterfront?"

Uncle Charlie shook his head.

"He's one of the few firms up for a bid to completely renovate all the buildings. We're talking big time here." Jim puffed up with pride. "Now I got a doctor and an architect to brag about. Not too shabby, huh?"

Uncle Charlie agreed and they threw a bunch of questions at Nick regarding his career. Inside, something shifted. He gave his answers but the strong wall around his emotions rumbled in warning. Jim spoke like he was no son-in-law, but a real son, comparing him to Lance. Maria made note of his favorite foods and pointed them out, smiling with pleasure when he almost blushed under her attention. Uncle Eddie invited him to his house to check out his new flat-screen television and watch the Giants, seeming genuinely pleased to gain another male in the family.

Needing a break to get his head clear, he excused himself and walked down the hallway to find an empty bathroom. On his way, he glimpsed a bunch of giggling women packed in the small spare room. Alexa held a baby in her arms—her cousin's, he presumed—and rocked the infant back and forth with a natural feminine grace. The women spoke in hushed whispers and he caught the tail end of "great sex" when he paused in the doorway.

The mass stopped and stared at him in silence.

Nick shifted on his other foot, suddenly uncom-fortable with the blatant looks of all Alexa's cousins. "Hi. Um, just looking for an empty bathroom."

They nodded but kept taking inventory. Finally, Alexa spoke up. "Use the one in the back bedroom, sweetheart. And shut the door, will you?"

"Sure." He closed the door on the tail end of another giggle, then the whole group broke into hysterics. Nick shook his head and headed toward the back.

He was stopped mid-flight by the three-year-old.

"Hi."

"Hi," he said back. Her wide eyes were serious, and he swallowed hard, wondering if he had to make conversation with her or if it would be acceptable to just step around and move on. "Uh, I'm just looking for the bathroom."

"I have to go potty, too," she announced.

"Oh. Okay, why don't you get your mommy?"

"She's not here. Have to go bad. Come on."

She reached out a tiny hand and he panicked. There was no way in hell he was going to take a toddler to the potty. He didn't know what to do. What if there was a problem? He backed off a few steps and shook his head. "Uh, no, Taylor, why don't you get Aunt Alexa to take you?"

Her face screwed up a bit. "Gotta go now. Bad."

"Wait here."

He turned and knocked on the door where the women were. Again, silence fell past the wooden barrier. "Who is it?"

"Nick. Uh, Alexa, your niece needs you to take her potty."

A pause. "I'm busy now, honey. Just go in with her, okay? It'll only take a minute." He heard a low mutter, then a cackle. Nick retreated, afraid to admit he couldn't handle it in front of a bunch of women who judged his every move. He turned back to the little girl.

"Uh, can you wait one more minute? Maybe Grandma will take you?"

Taylor shook her blond curls and jumped up and down. "Gotta go now, please, please."

"One minute." He raced down the hallway and into the kitchen where Maria was immersed in turkey stuffing. "Maria?"

"Yes, Nicholas?"

"Uh, Taylor needs to go to the bathroom and wants you to take her."

She mopped her brow with her elbow and resumed basting. "Can't right now; why don't you go with her? It will only take a minute."

Nick wondered what would happen if he burst into tears. The horror of the situation hit him full force, and he realized he had no choice or Taylor would pee her pants and tell on him and then he'd be in real trouble.

He raced back and found her hopping on one foot. "Okay, let's go. Hold it, hold it, hold it." He chanted the same line over and over as he slammed the door and picked up the lid. She lifted her dress and waited, so he assumed she needed help with her underwear. He closed his eyes and pulled them down, then lifted her onto the toilet. He heard a sigh of relief and a slow steady trickle that told him so far everything worked okay. His confidence came back. He could handle a kid. Nothing to be afraid of.

"I want ice cream."

Oh, shit.

Nick recited the same words Alexa had used that worked so well. "You can have ice cream after dinner."

"No, now."

He took a gulping breath and tried again. "You can definitely have ice cream. But just wait a bit longer, okay?"

Her lower lip trembled. "I want ice cream now. I've waited, and waited, and I promise I'll eat all of my dinner if you get me some now. Please?"

His mouth dropped open at her heartfelt pleas. What was he supposed to do? Nick reminded himself he was a successful businessman. How bad could a little girl be?

He kept his voice firm. "First eat your dinner, then you can have ice cream. You have to listen to your mom and your aunt."

The lower lip wobbled even more. Tears filled china blue eyes. "But Mommy and Aunt Al and Grandma never listen to me. I promise, promise, promise to eat everything on my plate, but I want some now. You can sneak it from the freezer and I'll eat it right here and I'll never tell. And you will be my best friend forever and ever! Please!"

He squirmed in pure terror and stuck to his guns. "I can't."

Taylor started to cry.

At first he thought he could do it. A couple of tears, he'd calm her down, walk her back to her mother, and still be the adult in this whole thing. But she opened her mouth and wailed while tears dripped down her smooth, rosy cheeks. Her lips shook and she looked so miserable Nick couldn't take it anymore. After begging her to please stop and she continuing, he did the only thing left.

"Okay, I'll get you the ice cream."

She sniffed prettily. Droplets clung to her long blond lashes and stuck to her cheeks. "I'll wait here."

He left her on the potty and walked back out in the hallway. He figured he'd meet a parent or grandparent or aunt along the way to stop him, but he just walked into the kitchen filled with chaos, opened the freezer, and found a Popsicle. Still he paused, awaiting discovery.

Nothing.

So, he unwrapped the Popsicle, grabbed a napkin, and walked back to the bathroom.

Taylor was still on the toilet.

He held the ice cream and she reached her chubby hand out and broke into one of the sweetest smiles he had ever seen in his life. His heart did a quick meltdown, and she stared into his eyes and promised him the world. "Thank you. You will be my very best new friend!"

Pride streamed through him as she enjoyed her ice cream. Kids were always hungry anyway, so he was positive she'd eat her dinner but decided he better tell her this whole thing was to be kept under wraps.

"Uh, Taylor?"

"What?"

"Don't forget the ice cream is a secret, remem-ber? Just between you and me."

She nodded seriously. "Emily and me have lots of secrets together. But we can't tell anybody."

He nodded with satisfaction. "Exactly. Secrets aren't told to anybody."

Someone knocked on the door. "Nick, are you in there?"

"Go away, Alexa, we're fine. Be out in a minute."

"Auntie Al, guess what?" Taylor screamed. "I got ice cream!"

Nick closed his eyes. Leave it to a female to break your heart.

The door swung open. Nick imagined the scene before her eyes. Taylor on the potty, eating an ice-cream pop, while he crouched on the small wicker stool in front of her, holding a wad of toilet paper in hand.

"Ah, shit."

"Shit. Shit, shit, shit," Taylor repeated happily. "See my ice cream, Auntie Al? I got it from him! My new best friend."

Nick waited for the explosion. The laughter. Anything but the dead silence from the bathroom doorway. When he finally got brave enough to look up, Alexa stared at him with sheer amazement, shock, and another emotion he didn't understand. Almost tenderness.

She cleared her throat and got to work. "You really did it this time, squirt. Have one last bite and give the pop to me."

"Okay."

Nick wondered why she didn't argue with Alexa, then figured he should be grateful. His wife deftly wrapped the leftover ice cream in a wad of tissues and buried it in the bathroom garbage. She nudged Nick aside, picked Taylor off the toilet, and took the wad of paper from him to clean her up. Alexa pulled up Taylor's underwear, straightened her dress, washed both of their hands, and did a quick wipe of her mouth to remove any evidence.

Then Alexa walked out of the bathroom with a very happy three-year-old and a confused adult. She squatted and spoke directly in Taylor's ear. The little girl nodded, then took off to join the guests.

"What did you say to her?" he asked.

She smiled with an experienced smugness. "Told her if she breathed a word about any ice cream, she'd never get any more from us. Trust me, the kid speaks our language."

"You're not mad?"

She turned to face him. "Are you kidding? You have no idea how many things I've snuck that little angel. She cried, didn't she?"

His mouth gaped open. "Yeah, how did you know?"

"Happens to me all the time. You didn't have a chance. Oh, one more thing."

"What?"

"I am incredibly turned on right now and will show you exactly how much when we get home."

Astonishment cut through him. "You're playing with me."

She gave him an open-mouthed, curl-your-toes, drop-dead, tongue-to-tongue kiss. Then pulled away with a sly smile. "No. But I'll be certain to play with you later."

Then she sashayed out of the bedroom, leaving him with a hard-on and a confused look on his face.

Women.

• • •

Two weeks later, Nick wondered if all power was lost once a man had sex with a woman.

His last presentation with Conte assured him a decision would be final by the first of the year. He squirmed the whole damn time he spoke with the man, who immediately asked how Alexa was, but thought he handled the situation well. The investors had whittled it down to Nick and StarPrises—a big company housed in Manhattan. He had one big conference to unveil his final model and design before Christmas. Thank God Drysell backed him hard, because they neared the final battle. Unfortunately, Nick had no clue which way the count swayed and it made him nervous as hell.

He longed to come home and linger over a warm, hearty supper; watch the Giants game; and crawl into bed with his wife. With full intentions of not sleeping. As he threw the door open, stomped off the lingering snow from his shoes, and walked in, he was wondering how fast he could eat, get the score, and then move on to the important part when he stepped in a pile of dog shit.

He roared in outrage and lifted his shoe. Italian hand-stitched leather now stained a darker brown than intended. His beautiful wooden floors smeared. The stench of waste instead of cooking. He was going to kill her.

"Alexa!"

She rushed in from the kitchen, flushed from either guilt or shame, then stopped short. A long skinny shadow lurked behind her. Nick's eyes narrowed as he took in the mangy hound dog that had haunted his dreams. And decided, sex or no sex, this woman was no longer in control.

"He goes. Now."

"But—"

"I mean it, Alexa. For God's sakes, I want that dog out of my house. Look what he just did."

She disappeared, then proceeded to clean up the mess

with a garbage bag and a wad of paper towels. He carefully slipped his shoe off and stepped around the pile while he watched her dive into the task and her explanation with equal fervor.

"Just listen for a second. I realize we can't keep him—I won't even try to convince you—but the shelter called and told me his time was up and he'd be put to sleep today. I don't know why nobody wants him—he's a lovely dog—and if we keep him for a day or two I promise I can find a home."

The shadow hovered by the kitchen, yellow eyes reflecting no emotion as the canine awaited the verdict. Nick made a growl of disgust. "Nobody wants him because he's the ugliest dog I've ever seen. He could be dangerous."

She gasped. "He's very sweet, doesn't even know how to growl. The shelter told me they found him on a deserted road with a broken leg. He was probably thrown from a moving car."

Shit.

"I know he's messy but I think he's smart and no one ever trained him. I'll keep him in the back room and clean up and I promise he'll be out in a few days. Please, Nick? Just give me a couple of days."

Irritated with her plea and his reaction, he took off his other shoe and walked over to the mutt. As if in challenge, he stood before him and waited for any sign of violence or street breeding for an excuse to throw him out.

Instead, he got nothing. No wag of the tail, no dropping of the head, no growl. Just...*nothing*...from a pair of vacant yellow eyes.

A chill raced down his spine and he turned from the dog, determined not to be affected. "Just a few days. I mean it."

She looked so relieved and grateful he began to wonder if he actually did have some power. Then decided to press his advantage. "Have you cooked dinner?"

"Almost ready. Salmon steaks with fresh vegetables and rice pilaf. The wine is chilling. Salad is done. You'll have plenty of time to see the Giants game."

He cocked his head, impressed with her full knowledge of what a man likes to get back when he gives in. He took the test a step further. "Think I'll take a shower first before dinner."

"I'll bring a glass of wine up for you, then. You can eat in front of the television."

"Maybe I will."

She rushed to take his jacket and usher him upstairs. Nick decided a few days with a dog would be worth her gratitude. With that pleasurable thought, he stepped into his bedroom and shed his clothes.

. . .

Alexa escorted her new temporary dog into the back room, which had been covered in old, ripped sheets she had found in her apartment. She set him up with food and water and placed a kiss on his head. Her heart dropped a little when she noticed he never wagged his tail. Not once. Something about this hound dog pulled at her, but she was content just to have bought some extra time to find him a loving home.

Now it was time to service her husband.

She poured a glass of wine and made her way upstairs. The sound of the shower echoed from the hallway, and her belly tugged with delicious anticipation. Already, a warm dampness seeped between her thighs when she thought of making love to Nick. Her nipples hardened as she opened the bathroom door to a cloud of steam and placed the glass on the sink. Then began to take off her clothes.

"Your wine is on the sink, honey."

His voice came out muffled. "Thanks."

She slid the shower curtain to the side, stepped into the large marble stall, and smiled. "You're welcome."

The man looked like he'd been hit on the head with a sledgehammer.

She took the opportunity to slide her arms around his neck. Slick, wet muscles pressed against her curves, and a map of hard ridges and hair-roughened skin made her crazed. She couldn't get enough of his body. She realized they'd never showered together before, had never gotten to that level of intimacy, but he seemed to rise to the occasion perfectly.

And literally.

Within two seconds, his erection grew and pulsed in demand, and he groaned deep in his throat and reached for her, his mouth coming down on hers to taste and claim and pleasure.

His tongue plunged in and out with little finesse, just raw hunger, and she dug her nails into his wet skin and slid as close to his soapy body as she could manage. The showerhead poured spray over them like a waterfall, and her hair dripped around her face as she frantically moved her hands over his body. She kissed him back hard, her tongue swirling around his, and then she pulled back and knelt in front of him.

"Alexa."

"Shut up." She opened her mouth and took him deep. The water beat down on her head and back, and she swirled her tongue around the ridged lines of his penis, loving his taste and his texture and the low curses ripped from his lips that revealed his pleasure.

He dragged her back up with frantic motions, moved into a wide-legged stance, and pulled her up toward his chest. He paused as he stared deep into her eyes. Then brought her down hard on his throbbing length.

She gasped. He pulsed inside and her muscles clenched in welcome. Fierce desire stabbed through her as he clasped her hips and moved her up and down. She cried out and bit down on his shoulder as the motions grew fiercer, and she threw her head back and shook out her wet hair and screamed as she orgasmed around him.

He followed her until she collapsed against him, her knees and legs trembling, and propped herself up against his chest, pressing kisses over him as she practically purred with satisfaction. He held her for a long time under the steamy sting of the water, and when she finally lifted her head, he smoothed back her hair.

"The dog can stay for a week."

She laughed and ran her fingers over the lines of his face, loving the way he looked when he relaxed and teased her, loving every stubborn part of this man who was her business partner and husband and so much more.

"I didn't do this for the dog. This was purely for selfish reasons."

"My kind of woman."

"I brought your wine. Dinner is ready."

He didn't say anything, just kept looking at her. Unbelievably, her heartbeat quickened and her nipples peaked. Almost embarrassed, she turned to go but he stopped her, and his grin grew lascivious as he slid one hand down her front and gently pressed one finger into her.

Her breath caught and she quickened as he coaxed the tiny throbbing bud to flower. She gripped his shoulders and shook her head in denial at the power he had over her.

"I can't be—"

"Yes, you can. Again, Alexa."

He plunged his finger deep, moved back and forth against her swollen lips, and her hips arched upward to take him. He grew hard and parted her legs and surged forward again. She rode him with a wild abandon she had never shown another lover, and later, when her body shivered with aftershocks, he held her, then turned off the water and gently dried her. His ministrations were tender, his eyes hooded as he seemed to withhold certain emotions from her. She allowed him his secrets and took what he gave with a greed that shocked her with its intensity. But he never had to know. He never had to glimpse how deeply she felt for him or discover the secret she had always suspected and now finally admitted to herself.

She loved him.

Completely. Every part of him, good and bad, her friend and lover and partner and rival. She wanted to spend the rest of her life with him, giving him everything, even though she knew he didn't want her. She crammed the knowledge to a secret place inside. Then realized she'd take whatever he gave, even though it would never be enough.

She kissed him once, smiled, and kept the sadness from her face. "Ready for dinner?"

Puzzlement flickered over his face, almost as if he knew she kept something important from him, but then he smiled back. "Yes."

He took her hand and led her out.

• • •

"Go away."

The dog just looked at him without expression. Nick peered out the window at the falling snow and glanced at his watch. BookCrazy had closed a few hours ago and Alexa still wasn't home. The roads were icing up, and the forecast stated they were in the middle of a pre-holiday blizzard. Everyone seemed overjoyed that it might be a white Christmas. Personally, Nick didn't care as long as they cleared the roads and the power stayed on.

He made a face when he thought of Alexa calling him a Scrooge. She drove him crazy with her love of festivities, decorating the house, insisting on a real tree, even baking holiday cookies. Which seemed to look better than they actually tasted. When he told her the truth, she'd thrown the cookie at him. At least the hound dog had cleaned up the crumbs.

Nick glanced over at the doorway again. The skinny canine skulked behind the corner and peered at him with those yellow eyes. The week was almost up, and the mutt would finally be gone. He didn't like the way the dog followed him around and watched his every movement. He didn't act like a normal dog who barked and wagged his tail and slurped water. This one reminded him of a ghost. Alexa forced him to eat, drink, and taught him how to be walked. The mutt went through all the motions but his eyes remained distant, as if waiting for the real truth to be revealed. As if waiting to be dumped back on that highway. Alone.

Nick shook his head, annoyed at the shiver that raced down his spine. He'd been having dreams lately of the dog Jed had made him get rid of, dreams that haunted him until he reached for his wife in the middle of the night to exorcise the lingering images. He found himself doing that a lot lately. Losing himself in her body, in her warmth and heat, until the deep chill he carried within himself softened and the sharp edges blurred.

The yellow Volkswagen pulled into the driveway and relief skated through him. She flung open the front door and stomped the snow from her boots, laughing in sheer delight as she shook the white flakes from her hair.

"Isn't this great? We're going to get another blizzard next week so we may have a white Christmas."

"Why are you late?"

"Were you worried?" She shot him a teasing look and took off her coat.

"No. But I told you last week you needed new tires on your car. Have you done that yet?"

"Not yet."

"You can't drive in the snow with bad tires. I told you to take the BMW and drop your car off."

She scrunched up her nose. "I hate the BMW; it makes me nervous. Besides, I've driven in worse weather than this with worse vehicles. Oooh, the fire feels good." She warmed up her hands and sneezed. "Damn cold, it just won't go away. Do we have any holiday wine for tonight? I think *It's a Wonderful Life* is on at nine."

He scowled at her obvious attempt to ignore his advice. "That movie is corny. You've been sick for the past few days. You need to go to the doctor."

"I have no time. Holidays are the busiest season at the store."

"I'll bring you tomorrow. Then I'll drop you off at the bookstore and take your car to the shop for new tires. You should get rid of that thing anyway. Just buy a new one."

She made a rude noise. "Okay, Mr. Moneybags. I can't afford a new car right now and I happen to like my Bug."

"I'll buy it."

"No thanks."

Frustration nipped at his nerve endings. She loudly proclaimed her motive was money for marrying him. So why wouldn't she take his money? He'd offered his free expertise for her café. A new car. A damn new wardrobe, though to him she'd look perfect in a sack. Everyone else grabbed at his money, which was the easiest thing to give. But no, not her, she refused to take a penny over what the contract stated and still managed to make him feel guilty. She drove him nuts. "You're my wife and I'm allowed to buy you a car."

"A car's not in the contract."

"Neither is sex."

He waited for her to lose her temper but she just laughed. Then sneezed again. "Yeah, I guess you're right. But I'll keep the sex and say no to the car."

He stomped over to her and the dog cowered. "Think of it as a gift, then."

"You can buy me flowers if you want, but I'm not getting rid of the car. Boy, are you in a mood today."

"I'm not in a mood." As he uttered the statement, he got even more annoyed. His denial made the accusation seem more truthful. "Why won't you let me do something nice for you?"

She plopped down on the floor in front of the fire, kicked off her shoes, and looked up at him. "Let him stay."

He played dumb. "Who?"

"The dog."

"I gave you time, Alexa. You promised he'd be out on Friday. I don't want a dog. I don't want him." He waited for the launch attack and steeled himself to win the argument by sheer rationale.

Instead, she nodded, her eyes quiet and a bit sad. "Okay. He'll be out by tomorrow."

The guilt gnawed at his gut. He wanted to grab the dog and drive him to the pound tonight. Instead, he watched his wife hold out her arms and begin to croon to the mutt. The ugly yellow hound inched forward until he paused in front of her. With slow motions, she reached over and laid a hand under the animal's jaw, stroking his neck as she murmured nonsense. After a while, the quivering muscles relaxed and his ears fell back. Within a few minutes, she urged the dog to lay down in her lap and she continued to stroke his coat, smoother now that she had bathed him, a little fuller now that she had fed him.

Nick watched the whole scene play before his eyes, a mingling of past and present, a battle between loneliness and the risk of pain. And for the first time in weeks, the hound dog seemed to surrender for only a brief moment, to let himself bask in the tender ministrations of someone who proclaimed to love him.

And Nick saw his tail begin to thump.

The tiny motion was lost on his wife, who warmed herself in front of the fire with two wounded, lost souls beside her. She gave for no gain of her own, no goal she needed to reach. Love was not a prize but something she owned inside and shared freely. Every night she took him deep into her body and held nothing back. The woman who was his wife was a fierce, proud creature who both shattered and humbled him, and he realized in the glimmer of firelight that he loved her.

He was in love with his wife.

The knowledge came like a tidal wave that swept him up and knocked him over to then rise, coughing and bruised, shaking his head as he wondered what the hell had happened. He stood there in the middle of the room as she ignored him, and he watched his life veer off the main highway to a road filled with rocks and brush and potholes. Staggered with emotion, he took a step back as if to retreat from the whole mess.

Son of a bitch.

He was in love with his wife.

"Nick?"

He opened his mouth to answer, gulped, and tried again. "Yeah?"

"If you don't want to watch the movie, give me another suggestion. I thought we'd get drunk in front of the fire and watch the blizzard, but if you're cranky, I'm open to options."

She was talking about movies and he'd just experienced the biggest crisis in his life. Nick closed his eyes and fought off the emotions that burned through the last crumbling wall and left him with rubble. As if the dog recognized a fellow war victim, he lifted his head and watched.

Then Nick knew what he had to do.

Too new to express his emotions verbally, too confused to see how he'd play out this new hand, those whirling, messy emotions exploded through him until he could only reveal them one way.

He crossed the room and knelt before her. The dog made a low mutter and moved from her lap to disappear into the kitchen. Alexa looked at Nick with a question in her eyes as he laid a palm over her cheek and studied her face. As if seeing her for the first time, he took in every feature and let himself fall into the abyss.

"I want to make love to you."

. . .

Alexa listened to her husband say the words and her heart stopped, then pounded in an uneven rhythm. She didn't know what was different this time, but she sensed they had reached a cross in the road, and he was choosing the path less traveled.

They'd made love every night since Michael's party, sometimes slow, sometimes hot and frantic. He whispered erotic words and compliments, telling her she was beautiful and he wanted her.

But he had never looked deep into her eyes like he knew who she was. As if the outside layers peeled off to reveal the ripe pulp of fruit beneath, Alexa felt exposed to him. She held her breath and waited for him to back away.

Instead, he cupped both of her cheeks in his palms and spoke directly against her lips. "You're my wife and I want to make love to you."

Then he kissed her, a warm, slow melding that heated her blood, like syrup being poured over hot pancakes, until her body grew pliant and her lips opened to him and their tongues mated in the ancient rhythm man and woman had danced for centuries.

He slowly pressed her back into the carpet and shed her clothes, pausing to taste and touch every inch of skin revealed to him with a reverence that excited her and humbled her and made her want even more.

With quiet command, he parted her legs and knelt, separating the folds that hid her sex with gentle fingers. And then he kissed her, using his tongue and lips to push her toward the edge, ignoring her frantic motions to pull him back up until she climaxed hard and arched beneath him. He caught her hips and continued kissing her, until a sob caught in her throat and she begged him, begged him…

He surged upward and paused at her entrance.

"Look at me, Alexa."

Half drugged, she opened her eyes and gazed at the man she loved with every part of her being, waiting for him to claim her, waiting to take anything he could give.

"It's always been you." He paused as if to be sure she heard and understood the words. Intensity gleamed within amber depths. He gripped her fingers, as if trying to speak beyond words.

"And it will always be you." He plunged and she cried out. Never taking his eyes from hers, keeping her fingers within his, he buried himself to the hilt and began to move. Every time he reentered, he claimed more than her body. The stakes had changed and he was going for her heart, as he continued to give all of himself, pushing her with slow, steady strokes until she hovered on the edge of the cliff. This time when she fell over, he followed, holding her hands the whole time he shared the journey. And when they drifted back, he gathered her in his arms in front of the fire, pressed a kiss to her temple, and lay with her in the delicious silence that settled over them like the lazy snow drifting to the ground. She realized something had changed between them, something he wasn't ready to say yet, and she held tight to the hope, even as she cursed herself for ever having a thought he could belong to her.

A while later, drowsy in the delicious warmth of his body heat, he whispered to her. "The dog can stay."

She roused herself for a moment and wondered if she'd heard correctly. "What?"

"It's my gift to you. The dog can stay."

Overwhelmed, she searched for the words to express what he'd given to her, and like him, found none. So, she reached for him again and brought his head down to hers and showed him in another way.

. . .

The next day, Nick looked at his very sick wife and shook his head. "I told you so."

She groaned and flipped over to bury her face in the pillow, then gave a hacking cough. "You're not supposed to say those words. I need more NyQuil."

He settled the tray of liquids including chicken soup, water, and juice beside her. "Hell, no, not with the antibiotics and codeine cough syrup. The doctor warned me. No more nasal spray, either. I read an article about it."

"I want my mother."

He laughed and pressed a kiss on her tangled hair. "You have the television and remote. A box of tissues. A romance novel and the phone. Get some rest and I'll be back soon."

"I have to get to the bookstore. Maggie sucks at customer service."

"She can handle it for the day. Think of all the men she'll charm into buying more books. Eat your soup."

She grumbled something and he gently shut the door behind him.

Nick jumped into the Volkswagen with an air of satisfaction. With her stuck in bed, he finally had the opportunity to get new tires and an oil change on her rust bucket. He'd personally escorted her to the doctor, gotten the prescription, stopped at the pharmacy for supplies, then settled her underneath the covers.

A piece of him watched the scene from above and noted he acted like a husband. A real husband, not a fake one. The worst part was the deep satisfaction the role gave him.

He dropped the car off, grabbed all the papers from the glove compartment, and settled himself to wait. He hoped she kept the history of the mechanics in the jumbled mess, and he began sifting through invoices.

The formal letter from the bank stopped him cold.

He read through the letter and noted the date. Over a month ago. Way after the wedding. After she had got the money. What the hell was going on?

His BlackBerry buzzed. Distracted, he picked it up. "Hello?"

"About time you took my call."

Memories from his past dragged him back. With long practice, his heart chilled, along with his tone. "Jed. What do you want?"

His father laughed. "Is that the type of greeting I'm warranted from my own son? How've you been?"

Nick dropped the letter in his lap and went through the motions. "Fine. Back from Mexico so soon?"

"Yeah, I got married."

Wife number four. His mother would pop out of hiding to make trouble—that seemed to be the pattern. Maggie and he were only pawns to make the game more interesting. Nausea clawed at his gut. "Congratulations. Listen, I gotta go, no time to chat."

"I have something to discuss with you, son. Meet me for lunch."

"Sorry, I'm busy."

"I just need an hour, tops. Make the time."

The warning pulsed through the phone. Nick squeezed his eyes shut as he fought instinct. He better meet him, just in case Jed had some twisted idea to go after Dreamscape and challenge the will. What a mess. "Fine. I'll meet you at three o'clock. Planet Diner."

He clicked off the phone and glanced back at the letter.

Why would Alexa lie about her use for the hundred and fifty thousand dollars? Was she involved in something he had never suspected? If she requested a loan from the bank for the café and was rejected, where had his money gone?

The questions whirled through his mind and made no sense. For some reason, she didn't want him to discover the truth. If she really wanted more money, she would've asked him to co-sign the loan papers and it'd be a guaranteed acceptance. What the hell was going on?

He waited for the car and took a trip to the office to stall for time. His quick call to check on her confirmed she'd be fine until he finished his lunch with Jed. Temptation urged him to ask some serious questions, but another part of him wondered if he wanted to know the truth. He may be in love with her, but the bottom line still hadn't changed. He couldn't offer her stability and children. Eventually, if she stayed, she'd end up hating him. Terror washed over him at the thought.

Jed waited in a corner booth. Nick studied the man who shared his blood. Money and laziness seemed to agree with him. The Mexican sun had highlighted his hair, and the deep tan that lined his face gave him a character he didn't really have. He was a tall man and wore his designer clothes well. Today he was clad in a Ralph Lauren red sweater, black pants, and leather loafers. His dark eyes held a slight sheen of alcohol-induced humor. Probably a cocktail before confronting his long-lost son. As Nick slid into the booth, he noted the similarities in their faces and bone structure. He shuddered. What he dreaded most in life was sitting right across from him. The possibility of becoming his father.

"Nick, good to see you." Jed reached out and shook his hand, then spent a few minutes flirting with the waitress.

Nick ordered a coffee. "So, what brings you to New York, Jed?"

"This is Amber's hometown. Came for a visit. I'm thinking of settling back in town for a while. Set up house. Maybe we can spend a bit more time together?"

Nick tested the spring on the box for any emotions but it held tight. Mercifully, he felt nothing. "Why?"

Jed shrugged. "Thought I'd hang out with my only son. It's been a while, you know. How's business?"

"Good." Nick sipped his coffee. "What did you want to talk about?"

"Heard you got married. Congrats. Love, money, or sex?"

Nick blinked. "Excuse me?"

His father gave a loud laugh. "Why'd you marry her? I married your mother for love and that ended in a frickin' disaster. Wife two and three were for sex, and that blew up. But Amber is all about the money. Money and some respect. I already sense this one will be permanent."

"Interesting theory."

"So, which one is it?"

His jaw tightened. "Love."

Jed hooted and cut into his pancakes. "You're screwed. At least you got a nice piece of the pie from Uncle Earl. I heard all about it."

"Don't even think about contesting the will. It's already done."

"Arrogant, are you? You know, I think we're more alike than you want to believe. We both like money, and we both like women. There's nothing wrong with that." Jed pointed his fork at him. "I'm not here to make trouble—I got my own fortune and don't need yours. But Amber has a bug up her ass about me getting closer to my children. I thought we could all do lunch together. You know, Maggie and you, and Amber's kids."

The ridiculousness of the situation caused a moment of speechlessness. Nick thought of all the times he'd begged Jed to have a lousy conversation with him, let alone a meal. And now because his new wife pressed him, Jed assumed he'd jump to experiment with a father/son relationship. A twinge of bitterness leaked through the ice. Too little. Too late. Even worse, Jed didn't really even care.

Nick drained his coffee. "Appreciate the offer, Jed, but I'll pass. Haven't needed you before. Don't need you now."

His father's eyes turned mean. "Always thought you were better than me, huh? The golden boy. Listen up, son, blood is blood, and soon you'll realize you're destined to make the same mistakes I did." He practically snarled his next words. "Wanna know the truth? I married your mother for love, but she only wanted my money. Once I sniffed out the truth, I was going to break it off but it was too late. She got pregnant. And I got stuck. With you."

Nick swallowed as the nightmare unfolded before him. "What?"

Jed gave a nasty laugh. "That's right, you were her desperate attempt to keep me, and it worked. A kid means child support and alimony for life. I decided to stay and make it work, but I never forgave her."

The knowledge made perfect sense as the pieces snapped into place. Jed never wanted him in the first place, nor Maggie. "Why tell me this now?"

His father smiled coldly. "As a warning. Watch this new wife of yours. If she married you for money and feels you slipping away, the "oops" will be coming. Mark my words. And then you'll be trapped just like me." He paused. "Because you are just like me, Nick."

Nick looked at his father for a long time. A tiny trickle of fear escaped from the box as he recognized the man who had fathered him garnered no respect from his own family. What if Jed Ryan was right? What if all these years he'd been fighting his genes, and his time was up? What if he was destined to become like his father, whether he took the short or the long road?

The past few weeks had tricked him into believing in things that didn't exist. Love. Truth. Family. Alexa had already lied about the money. What else did she lie about? A chill skated down his spine. What if she had been working a bigger plan the whole time he'd been falling in love with her?

The doubts attacked with a vicious punch, but he ignored them and held his head up. "We're nothing alike. Good luck, Jed."

He threw some bills on the table and left, but his spoken words mocked him with every step.

Because in his secret heart, he wondered if it were really true. He wondered if he were more like Jed Ryan than he thought.

Chapter Ten

She was pregnant.

Alexa stared at the closed door where the ob-gyn had disappeared. Yes, she'd been feeling a bit nauseous. Yes, she hadn't gotten her period when she was due, but easily blamed it on stress. The craziness of the holidays with her family and work and Nick. And why would she have considered the possibility when she was on the birth control pill?

The words from the doctor rang in her ears.

"Did you take any other medicine for the past month?" he had asked.

"No. I just take Tylenol when I have a headache…but wait, I did. I had walking pneumonia and I had to go on…" She trailed off as the knowledge took root.

The doctor nodded. "Antibiotics. Your primary should

have warned you it reduces the effects of the pill. I see this slip-up a lot, actually. Happy news, I hope?"

A longing welled up from deep inside and burst through like a starburst of emotion. *Yes. It's happy news.*

At least for me.

She climbed behind the wheel of her Volkswagen. Then rested both palms on her flat belly.

A baby.

She was going to have Nick's baby.

Her mind flashed back to the past few weeks. They'd grown closer, until the natural rhythm of husband and wife became second nature. Christmas with her family seemed more relaxed, as Nick had made a true attempt to enjoy himself. He made love to her with a passion that reached deep and grabbed her soul. She believed the walls slowly crumbled between them. Sometimes, she caught him staring at her with such raw, naked emotion, she lost her breath. Yet, each time she opened her mouth to tell him she loved him, his entire demeanor shut down like a robot. As if he sensed that once she spoke the words, there'd be no turning back.

She had waited for the perfect time, but now her time was up. She loved him. She craved a real marriage beyond a contract. And she needed to tell him what she'd done with the money.

Tension fluttered in her belly. He'd refused to marry Gabriella because she'd wanted a child. Logically, Nick was afraid he'd repeat the mistakes of his father. But Alexa hoped once he realized the baby was real, and part of him, he'd open himself up and finally let himself love.

She drove home in a state of excitement and anticipation. Keeping the truth from him hadn't even occurred to her. She expected a reaction of shock and a little fear. But her gut told her Nick would eventually warm to the idea. After all, this wasn't a planned event, so Fate had sent them this baby for a good reason.

Stubbornly, Alexa believed she'd make her husband happy. The news would force him to finally open up to her and take a risk. She knew he loved her.

She pulled her car into the driveway and made her way into the house. Old Yeller trudged toward the door to greet her, and she spent a good amount of time stroking his ears and kissing his face until she saw the healthy signs of his tail thump. She hid a smile. If only her husband could be this easy. A little love and patience, and her dog bloomed.

She walked into the kitchen where he was hard at work with dinner. The apron tied around his waist declared him CHEF OF THE YEAR, a Christmas present from her mother. She snuck up behind him and stood on tiptoes, squeezing him tightly and nuzzling her nose against his neck.

He turned around and gave her a proper kiss.

"Hey."

"Hey."

They smiled at each other.

"Whatcha cooking?" she asked.

"Grilled salmon, spinach, roasted potatoes. And the salad of course."

"Of course."

"I have news," he said.

Alexa studied his face. A gleam of triumph lit his eyes and those carved lips kicked up a notch. "Oh my God. You got the contract."

"I got the contract."

She let out a whoop and jumped into his arms. He laughed and swung her around, then bent his head and kissed her. The familiar warmth and heat coursed through her, and she dug her nails into his shoulders and hung on. When he'd kissed her deeply and thoroughly, he eased away and beamed down at her. Her heart pumped up and filled with so much joy Alexa worried she'd burst.

"We're celebrating, baby. We have an extra bottle of champagne from New Year's Eve chilling in the fridge. Let's get drunk and crazy."

She paused and wondered when to spring her news. A normal woman would wait until dinner was served and they basked in the news of the waterfront deal. A normal woman would bide her time and ease her husband into the idea.

Alexa admitted she'd never been normal. The news of his success bode as a good omen to spring her own news.

"I can't drink anymore."

He smiled at her and resumed seasoning the salmon. "Trying to lay off the sauce, huh? It's not this stupid diet, is it? Wine is good for the blood."

"No, not the diet. I was at the doctor's today and he said I couldn't drink."

He glanced at her and frowned. "Are you okay? Are you sick again? I told you to see my doctor instead. Yours is that weird holistic guru who likes to give out herbs and stuff. I had to practically tackle him to give you real drugs when you had pneumonia." He threw the potatoes in the roasting pan and drizzled them with olive oil.

"No, I'm not sick. There's something else he told me."

"Oh." He set the spoon down and turned with a touch of panic. "Baby, you're starting to freak me out. What's going on?"

His concern touched her. She took his hands and squeezed tight. Then spilled out the news.

"Nick, I'm pregnant."

Pure shock glimmered in his eyes but Alexa was already prepared. She calmly waited for the realization to hit him so they could talk. She knew Nick wouldn't give in to his emotions but remain logical and rational.

He carefully removed her hand from his and took a step back toward the counter. "What did you say?"

She took a deep breath. "I'm pregnant. We're going to have a baby."

He seemed to search for his words. "But that's impossible. You're on the pill." He paused. "Aren't you?"

"Of course. But these things sometimes happen. Actually the doctor said—"

"How convenient."

She blinked. He looked at her as if she'd become a two-headed monster. Unease trickled through her. She retreated from him and took a seat at the kitchen table. "I know this is a shock. It was for me, too. But a baby is coming and we have to talk about it."

He remained silent, and she gentled her voice. "I never

planned for this. I never planned to make this a real marriage. But I love you, Nick. I've just been waiting for the right time to tell you. And I'm sorry I sprung it on you like this, but I didn't want to wait. Please say something. Anything."

She watched as her husband transformed. The man she loved and laughed with began to recede. The distance between them grew with an arctic chill that caused a shiver to race down her spine. His face was carved in stone. And as she waited for his next words, Alexa suddenly had a horrible premonition they'd taken another turn in the road.

. . .

Nick stared at his wife. "I don't want this baby."

The crumbling wall of ice suddenly regenerated and slammed back in full force. The only emotions that seeped through the cracks were resentment and bitterness. Oh, she was good. He'd fallen hard for her act and now he'd pay.

She blinked. Shook her head. "Okay. You don't want the baby. I understand you're scared, but maybe with some time, your feelings will change."

The words Gabriella had spoken months ago taunted him. His father's same promise echoed in his head. He'd been warned Alexa would use any means possible to trap him, but he hadn't believed it. He'd fallen for her innocence and ended up falling for her.

He'd clearly warned her from the beginning, and stupidly believed she'd respect him enough not to try and trap him.

And now she loved him.

He almost choked on a bitter laugh. Since the moment he had discovered those loan papers and met with his father, doubt battled with his need to believe in her. So, he'd let the matter go and decided to trust her. To trust she'd tell him the truth about what she used the money for on her own.

But now she revealed her deceit, with her glowing face and eyes filled with triumph.

A baby.

She was having his baby.

The rage swirled up and encompassed him in a black, buzzing cloud. "What's the matter, Alexa? Wasn't the one hundred fifty grand enough for you? Or did you get a little hungrier along the way?"

He saw pain transform her face but now he knew the ruse and knew it well. Her voice wobbled when she spoke. "What are you talking about?"

"Game's up. You're a smart girl. The end of the contract is looming. Hell, we're already at five months. You weren't sure what would happen, so you had a little accident to cement the deal. Trouble is, I don't want the baby. So, you're right back to square one."

She leaned forward and wrapped her arms around her stomach. "Is that what you believe?" She took a ragged breath and her body shuddered. "You believe I did this on purpose, to trap you?"

"Why else would you tell me you're on the pill so I'd stop wearing condoms? You admitted you wanted money from the beginning, then conned me by pretending to be independent. Kept me off balance." He gave a humorless laugh. "Refusing the new car was smart. I bought that act good. But you were really holding out for the big time."

"Oh my God." She bent forward at the waist, as if in physical pain, but he stayed where he was and didn't feel anything. Very slowly, she climbed out of the chair. The glow was gone. Her face reflected a ravaged grief that made him hesitate only a second. Then he hardened his heart and made himself face the truth about his wife.

She was a liar. She'd use an innocent child to get what she wanted, and the only casualty would be the baby. He shuddered with revulsion at the way she still played the game, looking to be the victim.

She gripped the wall and stared with horror from across the room. "I never knew," she said huskily. "I never knew this was what you really thought of me. I thought—" She took a deep breath and lifted her chin. "I guess it doesn't matter what I thought, does it?"

She turned to leave and he flung his last words at her back. "You made a big mistake, Alexa."

"You're right," she whispered. "I did."

Then she left.

The door shut. He stood in the kitchen for a long time until he heard the quiet patter of feet. Old Yeller sat beside him, his yellow eyes filled with a quiet knowledge that Alexa was gone for good. He gave a low whimper. The house rang with an eerie silence. They were both alone again, but Nick had no emotion to cry.

He was glad the dog grieved for both of them.

Chapter Eleven

Two weeks.

Nick stared out the window in the kitchen. Old Yeller lay by his feet. A cup of steaming coffee sat at his elbow.

He wandered his days like a ghost. Work kept him busy, so he poured all his energy into his designs, then tossed and turned in bed all night. He thought of Alexa and his unborn baby.

The bell rang.

He shook his head and made his way to the door. Jim and Maria McKenzie stood outside.

Grief overtook him at their familiar figures, but he pushed the emotion back and opened the door. "Jim, Maria, what are you doing here?"

He assumed they came for one reason—to completely demolish him. He prepared for Maria's tears and pleas for his unborn child. He expected Jim to punch him and curse him for hurting his baby girl.

Nick straightened his spine and got ready to take it all. He was surprised they'd waited so long. Hell, maybe her parents' rage would help. He needed to feel something—he'd even welcome pain. Eventually, he needed to contact her regarding the rest of the contract and see what they could pull off for image's sake. He wondered what tale she'd spun to her parents about him.

"May we come in?" Maria asked.

"Of course." He led them through to the kitchen. Old Yeller slunk behind the curtain, still not used to unfamiliar people. Nick gave his head an absent pat before retrieving two mugs. "I have coffee or tea."

"Coffee, please," Jim said. Maria declined and they both sat. Nick busied himself with retrieving cream and sugar and tried to ignore the knot in his gut.

"I'm assuming you're here to talk about Alexa," he began.

Jim and Maria exchanged an odd look. "Yes. She's been avoiding us, Nicholas. We think something's wrong. She doesn't take our phone calls. We visited the store to make sure everything was okay, but she made excuses and shuffled us out."

Jim nodded. "She hasn't spoken to her brother or Izzy and Gen, either. We decided to come over ourselves and talk to her. Tell us, Nick. Are you two having problems? Where is she?"

The strange *Twilight Zone* feel of the scene made his head spin. Nick looked at the older couple at his kitchen table and wondered what the hell he was going to say. Alexa hadn't told them about the baby. Or their breakup. Obviously, she didn't know how to handle the situation.

Nick smothered a groan of agony. No way was he confessing what had happened. They weren't his family. They weren't his responsibility. "Um, I think there may be something going on at BookCrazy. Poetry night."

Maria clasped her fingers around his. The mingling of strength and gentleness made him want to weep. Her eyes filled with concern. "No more lies. You are part of the family now. Tell us the truth."

Her words shook the lock on the box deep inside him. *Family.* She still believed he was part of the family. If only it was the truth and his wife hadn't betrayed him. Nick bowed his head. The words burst from his mouth before he gained control. "We broke up."

Maria sucked in her breath. He imagined Jim glared at him with hatred. Nick surrendered to the inevitable. It was time to confess his sins. Every last one of them. The carefully planned ruse crumbled before him, and he realized he needed to take the leap himself. It was time her family knew the truth.

"What happened?" Maria asked tenderly.

Nick released his hold and got up, pacing back and forth as he struggled for the words. "Alexa told me she was having our baby." He closed his eyes at the immediate joy that sprung over their faces. "But I told her I didn't want it."

He lifted his chin and refused to turn away. The familiar ice wrapped around him protectively. "I warned her from the beginning that I can't be a father."

Maria looked at him with all the understanding in the world. "Nicky, why would you say such a thing? You will be a wonderful father. You are loving, and firm, and have so much to give."

He shook his head. "No, I don't. You're wrong." The words about Alexa's betrayal hovered on his lips but he bit them back. He refused to break her parents' hearts by telling him of their loveless marriage. "There are other personal reasons, Maria. Things I can't discuss. Things I may not be able to forgive."

"You're wrong, Nicholas," Jim said softly. "There is always room for forgiveness. If you love each other. I betrayed my children's trust. My wife. I ran and turned my back on everyone I promised to cherish. But they forgave me, and we are whole again."

Maria nodded. "Marriage is messy. People make mistakes. Sometimes we do terrible things. But the vows you spoke encompassed good times and bad."

Nick choked on the lump in his throat. "I don't have staying power. I'm like my father. He's on wife number four, and he only cares about himself. I can't stand hurting an innocent child. There's nothing worse than not being wanted."

He braced himself for disdain and shock. Instead, Maria laughed and crossed the room to take him in her arms in a tight hug. "Oh, Nicholas, how could you possibly say that? Don't you remember how often you'd sneak into my house to steal cookies and keep an eye on your sister? You are a loving, whole man and nothing like your father. I see this every time you look at my daughter, and your love for her shines from your eyes."

Jim cleared his throat. "You are your own man, Nick. You make your own mistakes and choices. Don't go blaming anything on genes or hide behind excuses. You're better than that."

Maria cupped his face with her hands. Her eyes reflected love and humor and understanding. "A man like your father would never have given us such a generous gift. The money you and Alexa gave us allowed us to take care of our children and keep our home."

Nick frowned. "Money?"

She shook her head. "I know Alexa said it was a condition that I never mention it, but really, sweetheart, you must know how grateful we are."

He played along, as his gut screamed the answer was the final piece to the puzzle of his wife. "Yes, of course, it was our pleasure. And you used it for…"

Maria tilted her head. "To save our home, of course. Now Jim and I can take care of the bills and the upkeep. We finally have a chance. And it's all because of you."

The puzzle lay before him in vibrant glory. Complete. The money he taunted her with had not gone to her business. She had lied and saved her family's house. That was the reason she married him.

She'd tried to get the loan on her own for her café but was rejected. And now he realized why Alexa had never told him the truth. How could she? He'd never offered her a safe place to confess her truth. She refused to let him pity her or her family, or even hold something over her head. She took care of her own, because anyone Alexa loved she fought for till the death. She was the most loyal, forgiving, headstrong, passionate woman he'd ever met in his life, and he was madly in love with her.

The truth pulsed in every muscle in his body. She hadn't lied about the baby. She hadn't tried to get pregnant. Somehow, it had happened, but she had been stupid to trust him enough to tell him the truth and try to explain. She actually trusted him enough to think he'd be happy about the baby.

And he'd betrayed her. Choosing to believe the poisonous remarks of Gabriella and his father over the woman who loved him.

For the first time since his epiphany, he wondered if Alexa would ever forgive him.

He stared at Maria. This woman had given her daughter not only the strength to fight for what she believed in, but a heart that gave love unconditionally. A heart he prayed would give second chances.

He thought of his father and his many women. He thought of how hard he had worked to avoid emotion so he wouldn't be hurt the way his parents had hurt him. The way their relationship had hurt everyone around them.

The lightning bolt crashed through the room and shook him to the core.

He realized if he kept pursuing the same path, he'd be exactly like his father. Nick crushed his fingers into a tight fist. By cultivating distance in his relationships to avoid pain, he created a man who was a shell. But those actions caused the woman he loved more heartache than anyone deserved. He was a gutless coward who hurt people because he only cared about himself.

Inside, the fear still clung to him with a stickiness he'd bred over the years. But for the first time, he wanted to try. He wanted to give her what she needed. He wanted to be a father, a husband, a friend. He wanted to protect her and care for her and live the rest of his days with her. Maybe if he gave her everything he had, everything he was, he'd be enough for her.

The final wall around his heart shook. Crumbled. And broke.

Somehow, Alexandria believed he was enough because she loved him.

His hands trembled as he clasped Maria's fingers. "I have to talk to her."

Maria nodded. "Go make it right."

He straightened his spine and faced his father-in-law across the room. "I screwed up, too. I can only hope she forgives me. But I'm going to try."

Jim smiled. "You will, son."

Nick glanced down at the ugly hound dog he'd begun to love. "I think I have an idea."

. . .

Maggie set down a steaming cup of herbal tea and whisked away the cappuccino that had taunted Alexa for the past few minutes. "No caffeine. Tea has antioxidants."

She gave a weak laugh. "Yes, Mom. But I don't think a cafe mocha when I'm this exhausted is going to cause any damage."

"Caffeine stunts the baby's growth."

"So does stress and not making enough money to afford a baby."

"Hmm, must be the hormones. You're definitely cranky."

"Maggs!"

Her friend tossed a grin and plucked the lid off the tea. "I just like to piss you off. Make sure you haven't turned into one of those mooning tragic heroines you like to read about so much."

"Screw you."

"Better."

Alexa looked up at her with genuine warmth. She was going to be okay. After two weeks away from Nicholas, every day became a trial of strength and fortitude she was too stubborn not to meet. She'd kept the news a secret from her family but planned to reveal the truth this weekend. Maggie would help her. And even though she hadn't secured the loan for the bookstore, BookCrazy was making a more steady profit. She'd survive.

Alexa repeated the mantra every hour of every day she spent away from the man she loved while her baby grew in her belly. He'd made his choice and she needed to face reality.

"The count took me to dinner the other night."

Distracted by good gossip, Alexa smiled and studied her friend. "And you didn't tell me?"

Maggie shrugged. "We clashed. All he did was talk about you. He's in love with you, Al."

Alexa laughed. "Trust me. There's no spark and there never will be." She clucked her tongue with interest. "You fought, huh? You may have finally met your match."

Maggie snorted. "That's ridiculous."

She pursed her lips in interest. "He may be the only man who can handle you, Maggs."

"Pregnancy has warped your brain."

For a moment, Alexa caught a glimpse of regret shimmering from Maggie's eyes. She opened her mouth to say something, but the poets lined up and took their seats. Moody music played through the speakers to set the tone. Lights were dim, darkness fell outside. A buzz of creative energy filled the room as the poets began to recite their thoughts and dreams into the mic. She clutched a notebook close to her chest as she watched on the sidelines and allowed herself to sink back into the comforting fold of images. She closed her eyes and let her senses take over, sharpening, judging, as pictures flowed through her mind like oils seep and blend onto a canvas.

There was a brief pause as the poets changed.

Then she heard the voice.

At first, her mind was open to the deep, gravelly tone of the man who read into the mic. As her heart made the connection, a breathless, nameless fear filled her. Her breath hitched. Slowly, she forced herself to look at the poet standing on the stage.

Her husband.

At first, she thought her vision played tricks on her. The Nick Ryan she knew did not exist on the stage. Instead, a stranger stood before her.

He was dressed entirely in Mets gear. A blue-and-orange cap was set backward on his head where stray blond locks escaped. He wore a Mets jersey, jeans, and sneakers. He held an orange chain in his hand, and she saw Old Yeller sitting beside him with a quiet dignity that bespoke of purebreds and not mutts. The dog wore a Mets bandanna around his neck. One ear crooked at a broken angle. His tail did not wag. Yet his eyes did not hold the haunted look she usually associated with her broken canine. Propped up in front of his two front paws, a cardboard sign displayed the words: COME HOME.

She blinked once, twice, then realized the scene before her was real.

Nick held a piece of ragged notebook paper between his fingers. He cleared his throat. She held her breath as his voice spilled into the mic and reached her ears.

"I'm not a poet. But my wife is. She taught me to look for the extraordinary in the simplicity. She taught me about emotion, and truth, and second chances. You see, I never realized a person can keep giving everything with no thought to take. Alexa, you changed my life, but I was too afraid to reach for it. I believed I wasn't good enough. Now I realize the truth."

Alexa closed her eyes in desperation as tears leaked from her lids. Maggie's hand gripped hers. Her husband wanted her back. Yet, to choose that road was like the famous poem, an unknown factor. She understood his darkness better, knew if she turned her back on him she'd be safe. She'd make it on her own. The darkness beckoned her like an old friend. In that moment, she had her own choice. And God help her, she didn't know if she had the strength to try again.

She opened her eyes.

Low murmurings and comments drifted to her ears. She stared at the man she loved and waited for him to speak.

"I love you, Alexa. I want you and I want our baby. I want this ridiculous hound dog because I've grown to love him, too. I also figured out what I don't want. I don't want to live my life without you. I don't want to be alone anymore. And I don't want to believe I deserve not to have you. And I swear to God, I'll spend the rest of my life making this up to you."

Her lower lip trembled.

Maggie's hand tightened on hers. "Do you still love him?"

She choked on her response. "I'm afraid I can't do it anymore."

Maggie's eyes burned with a fierceness that shot sparks. "Yes, you can. You can do it again, and again, and again. If you love him enough."

Her husband stepped down from the mic and made his way toward her. The carefully built wall rocked on its foundation. "It was always you. You made me whole again."

And then, he knelt before her and placed his hands against her belly.

"My baby," he whispered. "I was afraid I had nothing to give. But I do. And I want to give it all to you."

The wall trembled with a shattering force and crashed around her.

Alexa made her choice.

She pulled him up and stepped into his arms. He held her close, his mouth to her ear, his hands around her back, as he whispered his promise to never hurt her again. A round of applause broke the silence, with loud hoots and high fives.

Maggie grinned. "About time you came to your senses, big brother."

Nicholas grabbed his sister and brought her into the embrace. His face reflected a lightness and peace Alexa had glimpsed before but never seen burn bright.

"I hope you know I intend to be godmother of this baby."

Alexa laughed. "God help us all if it's a girl. She'll be dressed in baby leather and brought to underwear shoots."

"And if it's a boy, I'll teach him the proper way to make a woman happy."

Nick placed a kiss on his wife's lips. "Oh, you'll get both, Maggs. I think I'll take my wife home and start practicing on a second."

Alexa's eyes widened. "A second? First I have to get past the morning sickness and weight gain and labor."

"Piece of cake. I'll be there through the whole thing."

"Only if you wear that Mets jersey."

Nick smiled. "Actually, I've thought about your arguments on the subject. Maybe you're right. Maybe the Mets deserve another fan in their arena."

She lifted her eyes up to the sky.

"Thank you, Earth Mother," she whispered.

Alexa made a mental note to give the book of spells to Maggie. Something told her Maggie's life was about to change. And she'd need all the help she could get.

As if he knew what she was thinking, Nick kissed her. "Let's go home."

She wrapped her arms around him and allowed him to lead her back to the light.

Epilogue

Maggie

Alexa groaned and set the plate on top of her huge belly. Her obvious disgust with the ability to suddenly balance large objects on her body made Maggie press her lips together in a desperate effort to smother a laugh. Her best friend's frown deepened.

"Shut up, Maggie. I'm miserable. Why won't she come? Almost two weeks late and the doctor keeps telling me to be patient. I want her out. O-U-T, out."

Maggie grabbed the dish—scraped clean of cake—and handed her a glass of milk. The sight of her friend's discomfort lured her to fix it, but the only thing left at this stage was dessert and foot rubs. She'd even tried to buy Alexa hot pink flip-flops with rhinestones, but the space between her toes was nonexistent. She clucked in sympathy and perched on the arm of the slate gray sofa. "I know, babe. It sucks. I bet in a day or two you'll be holding her in your arms and wishing you had more time to sleep. I hear they cry day and night."

Alexa wiggled her swollen feet and sighed. "I don't sleep anyway."

"Poor baby. I got her a present." Maggie scooped up the gift bag and swung it in front of her. "Straight from Milan, from one of the top baby designers."

"You gotta stop buying her stuff, Mags. Her closet is already bigger than mine."

"Good, then I'm doing my job." Maggie watched her friend part the tissue and remove the black jeans, hot pink T-shirt, and matching leather jacket. The tiny leather boots were studded with miniature pink diamonds. "Do you like it?"

"Oh, my God, how cool! I cannot believe you found something like this in a baby size!"

Pleasure shot through Maggie. "My goddaughter won't take any crap from the other kids in the playground. We'll start her off early being bad to the bone."

Alexa laughed. "Nick, get over here and see what your sister brought."

Her brother walked in from the kitchen and picked up the outfit. A look of sheer horror crossed his face. "Hell, no. My daughter will not be wearing biker gang gear straight from the womb."

Alexa's eyes shot sparks of fury. "You will not insult your sister, or her lovely gift. I think it would be a perfect homecoming outfit to put her in."

Maggie settled back for the show. Her usually laid-back friend now had mood swings that scared even her. Hormones were a hell of a thing, but her brother seemed to handle it with aplomb—in fact, Maggie caught a twinkle of amusement at his wife's challenge. The back and forth battles between them reminded her of their childhood rivalry. Who would have thought they were each other's soul-mates the whole time? If Fate hadn't stepped in with a forced marriage, maybe they would've never gotten together. Of course, Alexa still insisted it was that ridiculous love spell, but Maggie just let her believe it. No harm.

"Over my dead body," he tossed back with a casual air. "She wears the little ducky thing we agreed on last week."

Alexa stuck out her bottom lip in sheer defiance. "If I'm pushing her out, I'm the one who's going to pick the clothes."

"Hmm, seems I hear this a few times per day. If I could have the baby for you, you know I would."

Alexa bristled. "Liar. All men say stuff like that."

Her brother threw up his hands in mock surrender. "Is there anyone who will stand up for me and my intentions? Someone preferably with testosterone?"

As if the Zeus himself threw down his thunder-bolt, footsteps echoed down the hallway, past the kitchen, and stopped right behind them.

Slowly, Maggie turned her head.

"Ah, *cara*, this time I think Nicholas means it. What man would not take the pain for his woman?"

Her skin prickled in warning and…something else, something she refused to name. Count Michael Conte closed the distance and clapped Nick on the shoulder. She tried not to roll her eyes at the smooth gesture, or his trademark smile. The comfortable look shared between them was purely male—one man rescuing another from a crazy woman. Not that Nick needed much help. Already, he reached out to help his wife out of the chair, murmuring some comforting nonsense, and smoothing her blouse over her swollen belly. The sheer tenderness of the gesture and the look on his face lashed at her like the slice of a whip. The old Nick was truly gone. In his place stood a man filled with love for his wife and unborn baby. A changed person, because he'd finally allowed himself to believe one other person in the world could love him for who he was, flaws and all.

Emotion clogged her throat, and Maggie fought the tide back with practiced ease. God, where was this ridiculous envy coming from? Nick and Alexa deserved all the happiness in the world. She needed to get it together.

"Why does it seem wherever there is trouble, you are right in the middle, no?"

The lilting Italian accent stroked her ears and other places, but Maggie refused to answer the mocking question. Why the hell was he even here? Their normal Friday get together with Alexa's family was tradition, and one Maggie looked forward to. Pizza, pasta, and Chianti. The host's house changed every week, but it was something important to her—a staple in her crazy life she clung to.

Until Michael Conte barged in.

Suddenly, he appeared every Friday night, with a cannoli cake and array of pastries as indulgent as his come-hither, black-as-ink eyes. He acted as if their blind date had never happened, and that he was innocent.

Maggie knew the truth.

The man was in love with her best friend.

Oh, he tried to hide it. But she saw the sweet glances he threw at Alexa. Heard his Italian endearments and rich laughter at pretty much anything she said. Frustration nipped at her nerves. No one even suspected, especially her brother. He got over his once well placed jealousy and opened his house to their new friend. Somehow, falling in love with Alexa made him believe again in people's good qualities.

Luckily, Maggie wasn't as blind.

Nick shot her a look of warning. "Maggie was always the hellcat in the family." His lips tugged in a grin. "I remember when Mom came home one night with one of her new boyfriends. He was drunk and mean."

Alexa frowned. "Please tell me no one got hurt."

"Only him. He liked to smack me around sometimes and Maggie was worried he'd slip into my room after Mom went to sleep. So she rigged a trap for him. Sure enough, one night he opened my door."

"What happened?" Alexa asked.

"His foot hit the trip rope, a wet mop flew through the air, and he fell down on his ass. Woke us up, and we both made a big ruckus, big enough for Mom to throw him out."

Maggie laughed it off and cut a hand through the air. "No biggie. I was bored and looking for a bit of entertainment."

Michael stared at her, one brow lifted as if trying to figure her out. Her skin warmed, then heated to a sizzle.

Oh, hell, no. She wouldn't let him get in her head again. Once was enough.

"Well, I think we've had enough excitement today. I better get going," she said.

Alexa sighed. "Yeah, I better get to bed, too. Or at least put my feet up and watch trashy TV until the acid reflux hits."

She froze. Her mouth fell open and a weird squeak chirped from her lips. "Oh, my God. I'm wet."

Nick looked down. "Babe, you spilled your milk. No biggie. I'll get you another one."

The realization of Alexa's expression hit Maggie full force. Her heart beat faster. "It's not milk, Nick."

"Oh." He glanced back and forth between them with a confused expression on his face. "What was it?"

Alexa's voice came out high. "It's time."

"Time for what?"

Maggie let out an impatient screech. "Time for the baby, you idiot! Her water broke! The baby's coming."

Like in a bad sitcom, everyone stood stock still, as Alexa panted in anxiety with a wet splotch over her pants. Then the room exploded.

Maggie and Alexa watched in astonishment as the men scurried around like Chicken Little had just declared the sky was falling.

Nick raced to the bedroom and came downstairs with the overnight bag already packed, then grabbed bottles of water from the kitchen, and blankets as if they'd deliver the baby on the way there. Michael punched numbers on his cell phone and told Alexa's mom to get to the hospital. Nick tossed

Michael the keys to start the car, like it was a blizzard and he didn't think the car's engine would turn over, even though it was a frickin' BMW. Michael disappeared, and Nick tore down the hallway, slamming the door to the garage behind him.

Maggie looked at her best friend. "What the hell are they thinking? It's not the fifties. You'll be in labor for a while."

Alexa sighed and rubbed her back. "When they're excited the blood kind of leaves their brains for a while. It's not their fault."

"I guess. Do you want to change your pants before you go to the hospital?"

"Good idea. I'll be right back. Stay here so Nick doesn't go nuts when he comes back."

"Okay."

Maggie began cleaning up the leftovers from the table, then watched as her brother skidded back down the hallway, eyes wild. "Can you feed Old Yeller and walk him? I just called the doctor and told her we're on the way. Thanks, Maggie, see you at the hospital."

He grabbed the bag and shut the door behind him.

Maggie stared at the closed door and slugged back the last sip of wine, wondering when he'd notice his wife wasn't in the car with him.

A few seconds later, Alexa trudged back down the hall in yoga pants and a T-shirt. "Where's Nick?"

"He left."

Alexa muttered something under her breath. "Are you kidding me? I'm in an *I Love Lucy* rerun! Remember when Ricky went to the hospital and left her behind?"

"Oh, God, I loved that episode. How about the one with the chocolate?"

Alexa laughed. "Yes! She kept popping the candies in her mouth because she couldn't wrap them fast enough. You gotta love Lucy."

"Definitely."

The door flung open. Nick and Michael rushed in, looking frantically around like they lost something important. Like a wife in labor. "What are you doing?" Nick yelled. "I thought you were in the car."

Alexa sniffed. "I had to change, and then we were talking about the *I Love Lucy* episodes. Don't yell at me or I'll have Maggie take me to the hospital in a separate car."

Nick's mouth fell open. "I don't want to talk about *I Love Lucy*! The baby's coming—let's get out of here." As if realizing he was losing it in front of his pregnant wife, Nick dragged in a breath and spoke calmer. "I'm sorry, sweetheart. I'm freaking out. Are you ready?"

A smile bloomed over Alexa's face. "Yes." She leaned over and gave Maggie a hug and a kiss. For one moment, their gazes met, and something deep and female and eternal passed between them. "The baby's coming," Alexa whispered in excitement.

Maggie blinked back sudden tears and squeezed her hands. "Knock 'em dead, babe. I'll be there in a few."

"Love you."

"Back atcha."

"Alexa! We need to go. Now!"

Alexa waddled away. Their voices rose and fell in one of

their ridiculous arguments, and then the house filled with silence.

The baby was coming.

Maggie pressed her fingers to her mouth. Things were about to change. An undercurrent buzzed through the air, stealing her breath and bringing excitement. Danger.

And fear.

"They will never be the same."

Her head lifted as if a wolf scented her mate. Michael walked toward her in that slow, graceful stride, as if toying with his prey. This time she decided to answer. "No, they won't. They'll be stronger."

His lip kicked up in a half smile. "Why does it sound like a threat, *cara*? Week after week I eat dinner with you, and you barely say a word. You study me as if I am about to steal the family jewels. You sneer at my presents to Alexa and Nicholas, and mock my endearments. So, now that we are finally alone, perhaps you will speak your mind?"

The anger hit and she embraced it greedily. "I know the truth, Count. Oh, you hide it well, and I've studied your moves. Waiting for opportunities to be alone with Alexa. Befriending Nick until he welcomes you as part of the family. I've noticed it all, and you won't get away with it while I'm around."

She gave him credit. He didn't pretend to be shocked, or jerk back with surprise. Something flickered in his eyes for a brief moment, but then disappeared. He cocked his head and studied her, his gaze freely roaming over her figure. "Is this what you truly believe?"

A hollow sense of victory shook her at his refusal to deny her claim. "Yes."

"I see. So it will not matter if I protest this statement, because you have already made up your mind?"

"Oh, you're good, Count. But I'm better. And I have more to protect."

An odd sense of pride filled his voice. "Yes, you do protect the people you love, don't you?"

He didn't give her time to respond. With a stately nod, he turned. "I bid you *bella notte*, *cara*. I shall see you at the hospital. Beyond that, we will have to wait and see."

Then he left.

Maggie stared at the closed door for a while. A quiet patter of feet echoed through the room, and as if he sensed her sudden need for comfort, Old Yeller took his place beside her. She stroked his head, adjusting his Mets bandanna, and let the peace of the animal settle her nerves.

Michael Conte wanted to play games. So be it. She'd do anything to keep him from hurting Nick and Alexa.

Anything.

"Come on, babe. I'll feed you, finish cleaning up, and then go meet your brand new family member."

Somehow, someway, Michael Conte rattled her mind, her body, and her peace. She refused to consider the possibility of her heart. Too many years and bad moments had only turned her into the Tin Man. She had nothing left to give.

Still, the memory of one of her favorite movies, *Mary Poppins*, beckoned. It was as if the winds were about to change and no one would ever be the same. Ridiculous.

She shook off the thought and got to work.

Acknowledgments

Writing can be a lonely business. Fortunately, the community of romance authors are giving, dedicated professionals who are always willing to encourage or kick your butt on a deadline.

Thanks to my Twitter friends who make me laugh and keep me social, and all the wonderful authors on the loops who take the time to help promote a colleague.

I'd like to give a special shout out to the 4BadMommies group. We all need a safe place to fall, and this group of mommies is the best. Wendy S. Marcus, Regina Richards, and Aimee Carson—you guys rock. And to last year's roomies at RWA National in New York: Abbi Cantrell, Maggie Marr, Maisey Yates—we had way too much fun. Let's do it again this year.

Continue reading for an exclusive excerpt from

The Marriage Trap

by Jennifer Probst

Book Two in the *Marriage to a Billionaire* series!

Coming October 2012 from Gallery Books

Chapter One

Maggie Ryan tilted the margarita glass to her lips and took a long swallow. Tartness collided with the salt, exploded on her tongue, and burned through her blood. Unfortunately, not fast enough. She still had a shred of sanity left to question her actions.

The violet fabric-covered book beckoned and mocked. She picked it up again, leafed through the pages, and threw it back on the contemporary glass table. Ridiculous. Love spells, for God's sake. She refused to stoop to such a low. Of course, when her best friend Alexa cast her own spell she'd been supportive and cheered her actions to find her soul mate.

But this was completely different.

Maggie cursed under her breath and stared out the window. A sliver of moonlight leaked through the cracks of the organic bamboo blinds. Another evening gone. Another disastrous date. The demons threatened, and there was no one here to fight them back until dawn.

Why did she never feel a connection? This last one had been charming, intelligent, and easygoing. She expected a sexual buzz when they finally touched—or at least a lousy shiver of promise. Instead, she got zilch. Zippo. Numb from the waist down. Just a dull ache of emptiness and a longing for ...more.

Despair toppled over her like a cresting wave. The familiar edge of panic clawed her gut, but she fought back and managed to surface. Screw this. She refused to have an attack on her own turf. Maggie grabbed the raw irritation like a life vest and breathed deep and even.

Stupid attacks. She hated pills and refused to take them, positive the episodes would go away by her own sheer force of will. Probably an early midlife crisis. After all, her life was almost perfect.

She had everything most people dreamed about. She photographed gorgeous male models in underwear and she traveled the world. She adored her trendy condo with no upkeep. The kitchen boasted stainless steel appliances and gleaming ceramic tile. The modern espresso maker and margarita machine confirmed her fun, *Sex and the City* status. Plush white carpets and matching leather furniture boasted no children and bespoke sheer style. She did what she wanted, when she wanted, and made no damn apologies to anyone. She was attractive, financially comfortable, and healthy, aside from the occasional panic attacks. And yet, the question nibbled on the edge of her brain with an irritating persistence, growing a bit more with each passing day.

Is this it?

Maggie stood and yanked on a silky red robe, then stuffed her feet into her matching fuzzy slippers with devil horns sprouting from the top of her foot. She was drunk enough and no one would ever know. Maybe the exercise would calm her nerves.

She grabbed the piece of ledger paper and made a list of all the qualities she craved in a man.

Built the small fire.

Recited the mantra.

Gleeful cackles echoed in her brain at the act of insanity, but she shoved them back with another sip of tequila and watched the paper burn.

After all, she had nothing left to lose.

• • •

The sun looked pissed off.

Michael Conte stood outside by the waterfront property and watched the perfect disc struggle to top the mountain peaks. A fiery mingling of burnt orange and scarlet red rose, emanating sparks of fury, killed the remaining dark. He watched the king of the morning proudly celebrate the temporary win and for a brief moment wondered if he'd ever feel like that again.

Alive.

He shook his head and mocked his own thoughts. He had nothing to complain about. His life was just about perfect. The waterfront project neared completion, and the launch of his family's first U.S. bakery would seize the place by storm. He hoped.

Michael gazed out over the water and took note of the renovations. Once a broken-down, crime-ridden marina, the Hudson Valley property revealed a Cinderella transformation, and he'd been a part of it. Between the other two investors, they'd sunk a lot of money into the dream and Michael believed in the team's success. Paved-stone pathways now snaked around rose bushes and the boats finally returned— majestic schooners and the famed ferryboat that gave children rides.

Next to his bakery, the spa and Japanese restaurant courted an eclectic set of customers. Opening day was only a few weeks away after a long year of construction and sweat and blood.

But La Dolce Famiglia would finally take her home in New York.

Satisfaction rippled through him, along with a strange emptiness. What was wrong with him lately? He slept less, and the occasional woman he allowed himself to enjoy only left him feeling more restless when morning rose. On the surface, he had everything a man dreamed of. Wealth. A career he loved. Family, friends, and decent health. And pretty much his pick of any woman he craved. The Italian in his soul cried out for something deeper than sex, but he didn't know if it truly existed.

At least, not for him. As if something deep inside was broken.

Disgusted with his inner whining, he turned and strode down the sidewalk. His cell phone beeped, and he slid it out of his cashmere coat, glancing at the number.

Crap.

He paused for a moment. Then with a sigh of resignation, he punched the button.

"Yes, Venezia? What is it this time?"

"Michael, I'm in trouble." Rapid-fire Italian attacked his ears.

Michael concentrated on her tirade of words, desperate to make sense between gulps of sobbing breaths. "Did you say you're getting married?"

"Weren't you listening, Michael?" She quickly switched to English. "You must help me!"

"Go slowly. Deep breaths, then tell me the whole story."

"Mama won't let me get married!" she burst out. "And it's all your fault. You know Dominick and I have been together for years, and I've been hoping and praying he'd pop the question and he finally did. Oh, Michael, he brought me to the Piazza Vecchia and got down on his knee and the ring is beautiful, just beautiful! Of course, I said yes, and then we rushed to Mama to tell the whole family, and—"

"Wait a minute. Dominick never called me to ask permission for your hand in marriage." Irritation pricked at him. "Why didn't I know of this?"

His sister gave a long sigh. "You have got to be kidding me! That custom is ancient, and you're not even here, and everyone knows we were getting married; it was just a matter of time. Anyway, none of this matters because I'm going to be an old maid and I'll lose Dominick forever. He'll never wait for me and it's all your fault!"

His head throbbed in time to Venezia's whines. "How is this my fault?"

"Mama told me I can't get married until you're married. Remember that ridiculous tradition Papa believed in?"

Dread slithered up his spine and coiled in his gut. Impossible. The old family tradition had no place in today's society. Sure, the legacy of the oldest son marrying first was prominent in Bergamo, and as the senior Count he was looked upon as the leader, but they were long past the days of a required marriage. "I'm sure there was a miscommunication," he said smoothly. "I'll straighten this out."

"She told Dominick I can wear the ring, but there will be no wedding until you marry. Then Dominick got upset and said he doesn't know how long he can wait before he starts his life with me, and Mama got mad and called him disrespectful, and we had a big fight and now my life is over, all over! How can she do this to me?"

Gasping sobs broke out over the receiver.

Michael closed his eyes. The dull throb in his temples grew to monstrous proportions.

He slashed through Venezia's wails with an impatience he didn't try to hide. "Calm down," he ordered. She immediately quieted, used to his authority in the household. "Everyone knows you and Dominick are meant to be together. I don't want you to worry. I will talk to Mama today."

His sister gulped. "What if you can't? What if she disowns

me if I marry Dominick without her approval? I'll lose everything. But how can I give up the man I love?"

His heart stopped, then sped up. For God's sake, that was a snake pit he refused to jump in. An intense family drama would force him to fly back home, and with his mother's heart problems, he worried about her health. His two other sisters, Julietta and Carina, may not be able to handle Venezia's distress on their own. First, he needed to get his sister under control. He clenched his fingers around the phone. "You will not do anything until I speak with her. Do you understand, Venezia? I will take care of it. Just tell Dominick to hold on until I get this settled."

"Okay." Her voice shook, and Michael knew that within his sister's normal flair for drama she loved her fiancé and wanted to start her life with him. At twenty-six, she was already older than most of her friends who'd married, and she was finally going to settle down with a man he approved of.

He quickly ended the call and strode to his car. He'd get back to the office and think this through. What if he really needed to get married to fix this mess? His palms grew damp at the thought and he fought the instinct to wipe them down on his perfectly pressed slacks. With work eating up every spare hour, he'd put finding his soul mate at the bottom of his list. Of course, he already knew what qualities he needed in his future wife. Someone easygoing, sweet tempered, and fun. Intelligent. Loyal. Someone who wanted to raise children, make a home, but independent enough to have her own career. Someone to fit perfectly into his family.

He slid into the Alpha Romeo's sleek interior and pressed

the button for the engine. The main issue flashed in vivid neon before his vision. What if he didn't have time to find his perfect wife? Could he find a woman for a practical arrangement to satisfy his mother and allow Venezia to marry the love of her life? And if so, where in Dante's Hell would he find her?

His phone beeped and interrupted his thoughts. One glance confirmed Dominick refused to wait to be soothed and was about to fight for his sister's hand in marriage.

His head pounded as he reached for the phone.

It was going to be a long day.

Don't miss

THE MARRIAGE MISTAKE

by Jennifer Probst

Book Three in the *Marriage to a Billionaire* series!

Coming November 2012 from Gallery Books